FROSTWORLD
AND
DREAMFIRE

FROSTWORLD
AND
DREAMFIRE

JOHN MORRESSY

DOUBLEDAY & COMPANY, INC.

GARDEN CITY, NEW YORK

Dedication:
For Glenn and Steve

All of the characters in this book
are fictitious, and any resemblance
to actual persons, living or dead,
is purely coincidental.

PROLOGUE

From the records of Sternverein Contact Command

DUNUOS SYSTEM: PLANET TWO

Gravity: 1.08 OES
Diameter: 13,100 k.
Rotation/revolution: 244.6 days GSC
Atmosphere: N77.86; 021.02; breathable and safe
Planetary analogues: Fode XII; Wodenhammar

First recorded reference to this planet was in 2388; first charting in 2469; first Sternverein mission, present. It is the only habitable planet of a five-planet system. Classify as frostworld: inclination of axis and eccentric orbit leave a segment of Dunuos II permanently facing away from its sun, receiving no light but the stars, and an equal segment under permanent sunlight. Heavy atmospheric blanket serves to moderate temperature extremes, but we estimate darkside and sunside to be permanently uninhabitable by any known intelligent life forms. The remainder of the planet experiences annual alternation of light and dark, with corresponding temperature variation. One continental mass extends into this area, and one island chain lies fully within it. We find evidence of intelligent life on the continent, along its major river system. . . .

Strongly recommend that a First Contact Mission be organized and dispatched to Dunuos II at earliest opportunity.

Vos Van Ellin, Mission Commander

Dunuos System Pioneer Mission, 2606 GSC

ADDENDUM: The name of this planet in the language of the dominant race is *Hraggellon.* Henceforth, this name will be used in all documents and records.

PART ONE: REBIRTH

Another race, the Onhla, is said to live in the regions known as shadowlands and frostlands, and to be able to survive in the perpetual darkness of Starside for prolonged periods. Little is known of them aside from rumor. They appear to pass youth and childhood in a near-animal state, often running with tribal packs of predators. According to popular belief, they have the ability to communicate with these and other beasts, and possess directional senses unknown to the other humanoid races of the planet.

At the onset of sexual maturity, called *haldrim*, their appearance becomes humanoid and it remains so throughout life. Legends mention a mysterious third life-phase. No evidence has been found, and accounts conflict. In our opinion, the third life-phase is simply a manifestation of an afterlife myth. [Analogues: the Fourth Mind of the Jait; Copus IX.] At present we cannot evaluate conclusively.

Eno Glaser, Tertiary

Second Hraggellon Contact Mission

I.

FIRST ENDING

Hult crouched low under the snow-burdened branches of a firebloom and peered through the teeming air at the distant gleam. The dark was still and windless. Snow fell steadily and met the ground with a soft hiss. Hult ranged closely and sensed no life nor any motion. He threw back his head and sniffed deeply. The cold air carried the unmistakable scent of Onhla.

The tormagon crouching beside him twitched an ear at the slight sound. From deep in its throat came a stifled whimper of impatience. Hult laid a hand on the broad flat skull of the beast and responded with a low growl. Not long to wait, he told his companion.

The other tormagons were moving into place. They might not be needed; Hult desperately hoped they would not; but in the wastes of Hraggellon, caution was the first mandate. Hult tugged at the tormagon's long mane and growled again. The beast grew calmer. Soon, Hult reassured the great hunter. Very soon.

From beyond the firesite came a howl. Hult answered it himself, and then on either side and all around the little patch of light there rose a sound that seemed to freeze the very snow in its downward path before ceasing abruptly. Absolute silence followed. Hult waited, allowing time for recognition and response. From the encampment there came nothing. Not a howl, not a cry. Again, he had found them too late.

The Onhla sat close together in a row before the dying fire, their faces turned to Starside, the Place of the Long Dreaming. All their food was gone; their tormagons had taken everything of use. The Onhla were partnered females and males. All of them, young and old alike, had jet-black hair streaked with a single broad bar of white, the colors of the tribe of Vodmar. Not Hult's tribe, but kin; they would have received him, partnered him, if he had found them in time. But he had come too late.

Hult had followed the Vodmar through the frostlands since the fall of dark. In all that time he had seen no trace of other living Onhla. More times than he could remember, or wished to remember, he had come upon little groups of Onhla seated cross-legged before dead embers, facing Starside. He had seen the last of his own tribe, the Bachan; the last of the Zabrosse, the Yapak, the Ibb, and all the rest; and now the last of the Vodmar. Always their pale blue-white skin clung taut and dry to bodies wasted by the shaking sickness.

There was no more room for hope. Hult knew now that he was the last Onhla alive on Hraggellon. The tribes were extinct, their long history ended. The last knot had been tied.

Hult pondered these things for a time, then he settled in the snow beside the gaunt body of a young female. The dreamfire still smoldered. He touched the white band at his wrist and the wristblade sprang free. Two cuts, to mix the infected blood with his own, and it would be over.

He felt a sharp tug at his fur cape and turned to see old Arll's muzzle and bright shrewd eyes.

"This is all I can do now, Arll. I'm the last of my people. No reason for me to live on," he said in the beast's language.

Arll laid a heavy paw on the hand that held the blade. He did not agree. This was not the way an Onhla behaved.

Hult weighed the old beast's utterance, and saw that it was just. He could still be helpful. He coiled the blade around his wrist and rose to his feet. It was not yet time, after all.

Hult stayed with the tormagons all through the winter, going far for game and shelter. A growing restlessness drove him to press beyond the old boundaries. When food grew scarce, he led them deep into the eternal gloom of Starside, where the wind never ceased. There they hunted the ice-skimmers, the slow bucdyne, and the tulk. The succulent flesh of the skimmers was a rare treat, enjoyed hitherto only when one of the timid beasts ventured too far from the bleak sweep of everlasting ice that covered the dark side of Hraggellon. Now the pack gorged themselves on the fat beasts until they were too full to move. Even the mighty tulks, their foreheads bristling with scythelike horns, immune to the stilling power of the Onhla, could not withstand the carefully planned attack of tormagons, and their musky meat was added to the beasts' larder.

Hult returned to the shadowlands with the knowledge that he had led his friends where no tormagons had ever hunted before, and had brought them back, all of them, loping proudly through the blazing early bloom of the firetrees. They were uninjured, unscarred, and their bellies were lined with unnumbered feasts. These deeds would make new legends among the packs.

But Hult was not happy. When the first light came, and the sky grew brighter and the air became soft and bore the smell of new life, he was aware of an uneasiness he had never felt before. The haldrim was upon him. He needed his own people, and they were all dead.

When his life had been a purposeful search, Hult had lived each day hungrily and looked forward to each tomorrow that brought him closer to his goal. But now the goal was unattainable; and yet his life went on, day by day, just as it always had. A life among the tormagons, a life of hunting and fighting with survival as its greatest good, was not enough.

Now that the winter was over, the tormagons talked of mating. More than anything else, this made Hult feel the separation from his own kind. He remembered the celebrations of his people, the time of Great Gathering that now would never come again. He could picture the riders, the cloaks of the women, the swirl of life and color, and could hear in the ears of memory the deed-songs and the chant of rebirth and the howling of the tribal beasts. It was at Great

Gathering, the time of peace and joy and new partnering, that the sickness had struck and slain all but one who bore the name and colors of Bachan. The other tribes, the Kleto, the Pator, even the mighty Zabrosse, had shunned him and fled. The others had always feared the Bachan and thought them aloof and aristocratic. Only the tribal beasts remained loyal.

And now he felt a revulsion for the tormagons. The prospect of going among the feeble creatures who dwelt behind walls, in the stifling heat of Brightside, was sickening to Hult. Yet they were more akin to him than the pack. Already, as his childish pelt thinned and his color deepened, he was coming to resemble them. He might lead tormagons, but he could never become one. He could not stay among them, but he did not want to join the humans. Nor did he desire to live alone in the wastes like the elusive gorwol. He felt himself trapped and helpless.

On his return from a long solitary hunt, old Arll drew him aside, the trusted Arll, first of his followers. Arll was covered with scars, slower now, but wise and shrewd in his observations of the ways of beasts and other beings.

They sat on a hillside, away from the others. With soft coughs and growls, Arll probed the troubled mind of the youth, and Hult explained his feelings as well as he could. The language of the tormagons was not a subtle one, and Hult, so long isolated, would have had difficulty making his confused, dimly understood sensations clear even in the human tongue. He threw his arm around Arll's thick, shaggy neck, and with much fumbling for proper sounds, he tried to explain his troubles to the elder beast.

Arll listened patiently and silently until Hult was done. His response was terse. In human terms, it was something to the effect that all cubs are alike, but an Onhla is an Onhla, a tormagon a tormagon.

"And I am no longer a cub, am I, Arll?" Hult said.

"You are Onhla, we are tormagon."

Hult thought on that, and accepted the beast's judgment.

Every creature belonged with its own tribe. It was true, and it had always been true. In time of need, an outsider could be taken in, and could serve well. Hult had led the tor- magons to new hunting grounds, and they, in turn, had befriended him in his growing time. But now they were done with each other. He could show them no more, and they could not satisfy his hunger for something at once un- known and yet remembered in the blood.

"Time for me to go, Arll," Hult said.

"Time to go," the beast agreed.

It was so. Time had come for Hult to divest himself of the ways of the pack and try to become human once again. It would be difficult, this he knew, especially so with no tribe to welcome him. Many trials awaited him. But the patience and self-discipline learned in the frostlands would sustain him. Much had to be learned, but he would learn it along the way. Now he must go.

He laid his hand on Arll's skull. "You are leader now," he said.

The tormagon rose from his haunches and turned to face him. "Blood must be shed."

It was the law and could not be disputed. Hult stood, pulled the cape away from his neck, and raised his chin high. He stood motionless, hands by his sides. Arll bounded forward, laid both forepaws on Hult's shoulders, and closed his jaws on Hult's throat. As soon as the skin parted, Arll sprang back.

Hult touched the breaks in his skin with his finger tips and extended the bloodied hands to Arll, smearing the beast's gray muzzle. "You have overcome, Arll. Now I go."

"Good hunting," the leader growled, then turned and loped off to join the waiting pack.

Hult did not look after him. He was no longer of the pack. That part of his life was over. He started through the for- ests, toward the sun, in the direction of the haunts of men. An old song of the Great Gathering came to him, and he sang it out in a rough unmusical voice as he walked on.

As Hult each day moved farther from the hunting grounds and closer to the dwelling places of men, long-forgotten memories began to stir within him. He had been instructed in the ways of the dwellers behind walls. Men, he knew, believed in goods and possessions, more than they could eat or wear. If he was to live among men, he would need these things, or the means to acquire them.

He remembered that gorwol skins were highly valued in the settlements, and so he set out to hunt them with all the skill he had learned in his years with the tormagons. He followed the elusive creatures for two full Hraggellian darks, hunting where no Onhla and no tormagon had ever hunted, and with good success. When he first ranged men, in a distant caravan still far beyond his vision, he carried on his shoulder a roll of gorwol pelts worth all the wealth of these travelers, twice over.

He decided to join the caravan. It would be a good way to renew acquaintance with human ways, and would make entrance into Norion simple and unobtrusive. He saw no need to inform them that he was an Onhla. His skin was reddening, losing its protective whiteness now that his youthful pelt was shed. In his haldrim phase, he looked little different from any ruddy-faced Norionite. Only the deltoid masses on his back marked him as Onhla, and they could be concealed.

He had seen the ritual often when he was a child, and it came back to him easily. He stood in the path of the caravan, arms folded before him, bundle at his feet, and waited for the outriders to approach. Only when three mounted men encircled him did he speak.

"I ask the protection of the caravan until we reach the river. I will earn my way fairly," he said. The words came easily, even after all this time.

"You return to Norion early," a rider observed.

"My work is done."

"What goods do you carry?"

For answer, Hult unrolled his bundle. At the sight of the ghostly, sparkling furs, the chief rider swung down from his haxopod to inspect them more closely. "These are gorwol pelts," he said in a voice gentled by amazement. "Four of them! I thought gorwol were extinct."

"These may be the last," Hult said.

The first rider lifted a pelt to the light with a care near reverence. It shimmered in his hands. "I don't blame you for wanting to join us. There are plenty of men who'd kill you for one of these," he said.

"They would be stupid to try," Hult said coolly, and all three looked at him. Expressionless, he returned their gaze.

"No need to worry," the rider assured him. "All honest workers in this caravan. You're welcome to join us, if you can help tend the mounts."

So Hult became part of the caravan. He did his work conscientiously and well. From his early days, he knew the ways of haxopods, and was able to reassure the irascible beasts and win their confidence as his people had done for so many generations. He did not speak with them as he had with the tormagons; haxopods were stupid beasts, content to bear burdens. They had nothing to tell him.

At mealtimes, Hult mingled with the other travelers by the fire, but he did not partake in their conversations. The stories that amused them he did not understand, and he did not share their concerns and interests. Some of them he thought little better than the haxopods; some, no different at all. He preferred to observe, unnoticed, all the doings of the humans, to listen to their speech, study their actions, and learn to make his way among them.

They came to within two marches of the river. The sun was well above the horizon now. Shadows were small, and the ground was softening. The river would be in full flood when they arrived. Even now, in the intervals when the wind died, a faint faraway roar came from ahead. Spirits in the caravan were high, and Hult felt more at ease among the other travelers.

He was on his way to join the others at the working meal when disaster struck. He felt suddenly weaker than he had ever felt in his life. He staggered and fell. Waves of pain and nausea swept through him, and he gagged and retched. He struggled to his feet, but his knees buckled under him and he collapsed full length on the wet grass. He lay for some time unnoticed, shivering uncontrollably, until his moans brought two men to him. They stooped over him, and drew back quickly.

"The shaking sickness!" one of them shouted. "The trapper has the shaking sickness!"

An uproar arose in the encampment. Men rushed to and fro, shouting to one another to warn of the pestilence among them. Hult's perceptions became confused and erratic. Figures raced by him. Beasts snorted and plunged in all directions. The very campfire seemed to engulf him, searing his flesh with its heat at the same time that a rising wind chilled him to the heart. He could not speak for the chattering of his teeth. His mind jumped from moments of clarity to dazzled flashes in which he saw impossible things: men and women moved at blurring speed, or as slowly as if they forced their way through heavy snowdrifts; darks and lights succeeded one another as rapidly as the waving of a hand before his eyes; gorwols encircled him, seeking revenge for their hunted brothers; other creatures lurked in the forests, awaiting their chance to snatch at him; and sometimes all became one lowering, shadowy, formless entity, pressing in, smothering, crushing him with an oppressive but intangible weight.

And then he awoke, weak but recovered. His mind was clear. He lay on a dirty blanket he had never seen before. Beside him stood an empty water jug and some hard dry strips of meat. Nothing and no one else was to be seen. He struggled to his feet and tried to remember.

Slowly, confusedly, the memories came back. Frightened people, shrinking from one who carried the disease that had emptied whole regions and destroyed the tribes. Men speaking softly, just out of earshot, and a quick hand snatching away the roll of gorwol pelts while he trembled helplessly

and moaned for something to moisten his throat. The sound
of men and beasts and wagons moving off, and then the long
silence.

He seized the water jug, raised it, and dashed it to the
ground in frustration; then he remembered the water
nearby. He drank deeply, and began to chew at the tough
strips of meat. The sickness was gone now. His strength
would return. And he had learned his first costly lesson of
the ways of men: the weak receive no mercy.

Hult traveled the rest of the way alone, unhurried, and
entered Norion at the very fall of dark. He found work at
the stable of an inn on the edge of the city. He was near the
riverside quays and the outer shell; the sense of enclosure
was not so oppressive here as it would have been deeper in
Norion.

Hult did his work well and spoke to no one. If any looked
too closely at him, he ducked his head and hid among the
animals. He kept the silky hair below his eyes cropped short,
and covered his back at all times. To any casual observer, he
looked to be an ordinary resident of Norion. Few of the
guests came near him, and those who did recoiled at once
from the animal stench that reeked from him, strong even
for the insensitive dwellers in the closed city.

Hult bided his time. He saw merchants, traders, herds-
men, peddlers, and occasional otherworlders in strange
dress, speaking the common tongue with unfamiliar accents.
He listened, and pondered, and his observations all led him
to one conclusion: the shrewdness, cunning, and patience
that had served him so well among the tormagons were
equally useful attributes among men. He awaited only the
opportunity to use them.

Hult had been nearly two darks at the inn when he overheard a conversation that made him think deeply about his
future. Two merchants seated themselves in the warming
room, on the slab bench by the fire, to discuss business mat-

ters while digesting their meal. Hult had learned much from such idle conversations, so he moved close to them, staying in the shadows, and listened intently to their words. At first they spoke unhappily about the poor state of things in general, each seeking to outdo the other in prophecies of imminent ruin, and Hult decided that there was little to gain from them. He was on the point of slipping away when a reference to the fur trade made him stay.

"Nine darks since I've bought or sold a gorwol pelt, and nearly that long for a good tormagon. Gorwol used to be the most popular fur I had, and now there isn't one to be had on the planet," one merchant lamented.

"We'll never see one again. All the trappers are dead," said his companion.

"I don't regret the passing of the Onhla. They always made me feel uneasy."

"I never liked them much myself. I could never be sure whether they were animal or human . . . really human. They can speak to beasts, you know. I've seen them do it."

"But they were the only ones who brought in gorwol pelts."

They were silent for a time, then the first merchant said, "There were some fine ones came in with a caravan just before . . . oh, I guess about two darks ago. Did you see them?"

"Magnificent. Best I've ever seen. The trailmaster said he took them off a dead man."

The first merchant chuckled at the explanation. "I'll bet they're not the first pelts he took off a dead man."

"That's the chance they take. It's rough going out there. If the beasts don't get you, your friends will. Did you ever think that the dead man might have been the last tribesman on Hraggellon?"

"He didn't say it was a tribesman, did he? I heard that he took them from a dead trapper, that's all."

The second merchant's voice was thoughtful. "The trapper died of the shaking sickness, that's what he said. And it was the shaking sickness that wiped out the tribesmen. Even with that, the pelts went for a fortune."

"Why wouldn't they? Gorwol pelts can be washed, and they may be the last we'll ever see. The Onhla are gone, and the gorwol are gone, too." The first merchant sighed. "I don't know what we'll do now."

Hult stole away and hid himself in the farthest part of the stables. He needed time to think on what he had learned.

The merchants were wrong. Gorwol still lived, but the way to them lay through Starside, beyond the reach of any but an Onhla. This Hult knew, for he had seen them and hunted them.

Those thick, shimmering silver furs had always been valued in Norion, as much for their rarity as for their beauty. None but Onhla could provide them, for none but Onhla could endure the cold long enough to reach the gorwol's habitat and return. But the Onhla did not hunt for the pleasure of others. They hunted for food, not wealth. A nomadic people, they cared little for wealth or goods and scorned bargaining and bartering. More often than not, the pelts that came to Norion came as gifts; had Hult retained his, he would have sold them for the first offer and been happy to have the distasteful business over with.

But now he thought of wealth and what it might enable him to do. He recalled an old tale of the Onhla, familiar to him from his earliest days among the tribe. Before this he had not believed it; now he had no other solace.

It was said among the tribes that, long ago, some Onhla had been taken to a place named Insgar. No one knew where Insgar was, or why they had gone. This was never said. All anyone knew was that Insgar was far away, somewhere beyond the stars, and no one had ever gone there and returned. Otherworlders might have gone there in their great vessels, but never had an Onhla returned.

It was much to ponder.

Hult had never actually seen a driveship, but during his stay at the inn he had heard of them. They were great machines that lifted otherworlders from the ground beneath their feet and hurled them upward. Once aloft, they traveled at great speed to other worlds like Hraggellon. Such other worlds existed, Hult knew, for the knots of the Maker of Weathers, and of First-Breath, told of them, and the knots did not lie.

And still, in all the history of the Onhla, no tribesman had ever ridden in one of those machines and told of it afterward. The tale of Insgar was a dubious one, not a true legend preserved in the knots. Onhla did not need or want the other worlds. They had a good world, good partners and hunting beasts, and felt no desire to walk through strange weathers or hunt in unfamiliar forests. Such were not their ways.

But if one were the last Onhla, one had other duties. Hult understood them only faintly now, and was confused. They seemed to bind him to the planet at the same time they urged him outward. He thought of the dreamers, forever unheeded because their last hope had fled to another world; and then he thought of the duty of restoration. The old saying was clear: "In the beginning, hunter; in the midlight, guide and progenitor; then the gathering dark and the long dream." For the few, new life and new wisdom followed the haldrim. But that happened rarely, and the way was painful. Better to fulfil one's duties and hope for a long and peaceful dreamtime.

He was in haldrim now, and his duty was to create a new tribe. To do this, he had to find an Onhla partner. The pelts of the gorwol could buy him passage anywhere, and bring him back to Hraggellon. If there were indeed lost Onhla on Insgar—on any world—he would find them and bring them back to the homeworld where they belonged. There would be a new beginning.

It must be done, and only Hult could do it.

RECOMMENDATIONS, SECTION 3:

A. that the Sternverein take immediate advantage of the volatile political situation to establish a binding and enforceable trade agreement;

B. that for this purpose an experienced trader be ordered to Hraggellon at once and

    i. authorized to enter into official and unofficial agreements, as the situation suggests, and

    ii. assigned one assistant whose confidential duty shall be to cultivate the rulers of Norion;

C. that to dispel the natural suspicions of the Norionites, security forces on this mission be held to the minimum, and sequestered aboard ship until needed; and consequently,

D. that all personnel involved be expendable.

Havers Ruysche, Primary

Fifth Hraggellon Mission

II.

THE SIXTH HRAGGELLON MISSION

Norion stank. It had come a long way in recent times; nonetheless, it stank. Certainly, it was the center of such civilization and progress as Hraggellon could boast. But Seb Dunan had seen too many worlds to be easily impressed. Norion had a long way to go before Dunan could bring himself to dignify it with the name of city.

Seb Dunan was surfeited with far worlds and strange places. He had reveled in the maternal city of Tarquin VII on the feast of Landfall, traded on dreary Tricaps and in the headquarters of the flourishing Planetary League on Mazat, and listened to the wind in the towers of silent Hovonor. He had known scores of worlds, visited bustling young towns and cities long dead, seen splendor and squalor in close communion. To him, Norion was no more than a rude outpost on a barbaric world, a glorified trading post with a nasty smell to it, an overgrown burrow where unwashed humanoids in unwashed furs huddled in quarrelsome refuge from a murderous climate.

But it was a challenge. More important, it was a chance; and not without interesting features. Out in the cold reaches of Starside dwelt fur-bearing creatures with pelts unlike anything on the known worlds. Valuable beyond imagining, they were. It was said that one of the Trulban tyrants had sold four thousand of his subjects into slavery for the price of a coronation robe of gorwol skins. Dunan did not believe the tale, but all the same, it made one think. Shouldn't be surprised if it turned out to be true, though, he reflected. Trulbans are a daft lot. So are tyrants.

And Hraggellon had other items of potential value as well. Those light-globes, certainly. "Tears of Yadd" the natives called them. The earlier contact teams hadn't even mentioned them. But they hadn't mentioned the stink of Norion in darktime, either. Seb Dunan wondered if the globes had a religious significance. That could make it hard to trade for them. Problem there, perhaps, but he could find a way around it. There was a way around everything.

He lay supine on the sleeping platform, frowning slightly, hands folded over his ample belly, body relaxed, mind working at its customary speed. He foresaw potential difficulties, but nothing he could not overcome. The people of Norion were a dull bunch. Thick as Quespodons, the lot of them. No wonder they fell on their knees when the first other-worlders landed. Must have thought they were gods. Soon learned otherwise, Dunan thought, with a quiet little sniff of dry laughter. Still, even these people may have been different under other circumstances. A world like Hraggellon can wear a race down, erode the civilizing instincts. He recalled the old saying on Toxxo: "Hard worlds make hard races." Can't dispute that. As a corollary, *smelly races make smelly cities* was equally true. He took a deep inhalation from his scent-case and felt better.

Something had certainly made a hard race of the Onhla, if the tales he heard were to be credited. Hunting in Starside, where the cold could freeze the blood in an ordinary man's veins before he went fifty paces. Dunan pondered that and shuddered. Glad I'm dealing with the townsmen, he thought gratefully. No hunting for me, not if I can help it. I'll get my skins from a merchant here, whatever his price. I'll get all the Tears of Yadd that I need right here in Norion, too.

He had not had a chance to examine one of the light-globes closely before this. He sat up on the sleeping platform and gingerly touched his finger tips to the glowing sphere cupped in its bracket on the wall. It gave off no heat. He lifted it, and it came away in his hand, still glowing. He sniffed at its surface, then held the globe close to his ear, shook it, and listened. He ran his fingers over the smooth uneven surface. All his investigation told him nothing. No smell, no sound, no peculiarities of texture. What powered the thing, and how it was made, eluded him. The light-globes were natural objects, of that he was almost certain. What if they were a life-form? That could present a problem —in price, if nothing else.

He turned the globe in his hands, and its light grew brighter. Turning it again, in a different direction, he reduced the light. After a few trials, he found he could control the intensity, even though he did not understand the mechanism. That certainly made a natural origin less likely. It was a puzzle.

Puzzle or not, the globe was useful. He brought it to full brightness and raised it overhead to take his first close look at the sleeping chamber.

It was a square room, about six meters to a side, with a low ceiling. Dunan was not a tall man, but if he had extended his arm full length, the light-globe in his hand would have touched overhead. The door was barely head-high, and tightly shut. Narrow slits in the wall opposite provided all the ventilation; they were sealed now against the pundergorn, the hard darktime wind that roared down the long valley of the Moharil. A pair of cylindrical baskets for his belongings completed the furnishings.

Dunan dimmed the light and returned it to its bracket. He lay back cautiously on the sleeping platform, a chill slab as hard and unyielding as the outer plates of a driveship, and told himself that there was no use complaining. Whatever its shortcomings, this was probably one of the best sleeping chambers in Norion. Private, at least, and privacy was rare here in darktime. But such was the life of a trader, and none knew that better than Seb Dunan. He would not have used this room to quarter livestock, but by local standards, it was luxurious.

Hraggellians certainly were a strange lot. They were a husky folk, built much like Skeggjatts, and they spent all of darktime indoors—the townsmen did, at any rate—and yet their interiors were cheerless, cavelike, absolutely naked of adornment. Perhaps it was nostalgia for primitive times.

Couldn't have been too long ago that they were troglodytes, to judge from their current social graces. Dumb brutes, all of them. Even the Remembrancers were no more than a notch above barbarity. All memory, and not much of anything else.

A good trade item occurred to him and he recorded it at once, along with his observations on the Tears of Yadd. These people would surely go mad for motion paintings. Not the genuine article, of course. Be wasted on this lot, even if they could be obtained, Dunan thought. We'll use the imitations. Not nearly as smooth, but they'll impress Hraggellians.

He remembered the breathtaking wall-sized motion paintings he had seen on Barbary, work of the k'Turalp'Pa at their artistic height. No more of those being made. Whole race dying out, from what I hear. No wonder, with a name like that, he thought, laughing that dry inward laugh of his. Can't even pronounce it properly themselves.

He raised his head and studied the blank wall opposite his sleeping platform. A motion painting right there would put some life into this room. A festival scene from one of the primitive cultures, say, or a season-change sequence. That's what this place needs—life and color. Something to lift the spirits. The forest cities of Feofor would do nicely; their year-cycle just about matched Hraggellon's.

Norion, on the whole, impressed Dunan as a convalescent emerging from a near-fatal illness. It faced a long and painful recovery, and needed all the help it could get. Dunan was not optimistic about its prospects. Even in normal times, the harsh climate and unrelenting winds kept the Hraggellians scrabbling merely to survive. Now, after famine, plague, and a long struggle among the ruling families, they seemed to be a depleted race. No time to think of improving their city. Or themselves.

A gloomy thought. Dunan snapped open the cover of his scent-case and raised it to his nostrils. After a few deep breaths he felt much better; full of energy, in fact, and eager to see something more of the caravansary where their cautious hosts had lodged them. He had not been welcomed to Norion. Far from it. Seb Dunan and his assistant had dragged themselves in through a battering wind, like poor relations coming to beg. "Orm the Peacebringer" he might be, but the new ruler of Hraggellon would never be called "Orm the Hospitable." Not by Seb Dunan.

But while he had not been welcomed, he had not been told to stay put. That was his own idea, this patient waiting for some representative of Orm to come and offer greetings. More than likely, such amenities had never been heard of on Hraggellon. He could rot here, waiting for a civil reception. Lie here talking to himself until the coming of light, and accomplish nothing. No sense in that. Like all starfarers, he talked to himself far too much. He had been his own sole company for too long.

It was time to start moving, he told himself, rising and selecting a warm outer robe. See what they've got here and what they need. That's what I'm here to do.

As he drew the robe close about him, the clinger began to glow, brightening quickly to a pale green ringed with amethyst. These little beauties were a find: utterly harmless, striking to look at, and a perfect pet. Beetlelike, sentient, they lived on air and an occasional drop of water, and glowed like a tiny star in proximity to human body heat. The stringy burntland digger who had sold it to Dunan had told a wild story of the clinger's power to confer great sexual prowess on the wearer. A lie, of course, but a good one. It would be a sure selling point on the effete inner worlds.

The caravansary was U-shaped, with its rounded end turned to the full force of the pundergorn. Dunan left his chamber, walked the long way around the narrow gallery, and descended the ramp to the great arcade that was the backbone of Norion. Here the noise of strollers and vendors drowned out the incessant wind drone, and one could enjoy an illusion of warmth, provided one moved at a brisk pace and stopped often to make use of a vendor's fire.

The dome was an impressive achievement, especially for a world that was so primitive in most other respects; Dunan had to admit that much. It must have reached close to 120 meters at its highest point, and 250 at its widest. Total length was hard to estimate, but Dunan put it at no less than 800 meters, possibly a good bit more. The structure was completely cantilevered, and it withstood a steady wind of as much as force thirty for a full darktime.

If they can do that, Dunan thought, glancing upward, you'd think they'd have found a better way of travel than footpower and muscle. Then again, where would they go? Maybe they aren't such fools after all. What good is transportation on a world where there's no place to go?

The arcade was almost pleasant. Darktime had just passed the midpoint, warmth and light were coming, and the spirits of the Hraggellians showed signs of rising from the darktime ebb, time of the madness they called memur. Here and there, Dunan saw an expression close to a smile. Understandable how this cold and dark and endless roaring wind would wear you down, he reflected. Wouldn't want a lifetime of it myself. A wonder they're not all a lot madder.

But soon the wind would shift, the rivers would flow again, and the lands around Norion would come alive until the next fall of darkness. By then, his work would be done. And then, for all Seb Dunan cared, Hraggellon could freeze solid.

He made frequent stops, as much out of genuine interest as from the need for warmth and conversation. He had been a starfaring trader all his life, and the sight of a market stirred his blood even now. He stopped at a food stall, sniffed and tasted, but ate only a bite. Hraggellian food was too heavily and strangely spiced for his taste or his aging stomach. He inspected tools and weapons, haggled spiritedly over a pair of boots but did not buy them, and came at last to a fur-merchant's alcove. Here he stopped long.

A dozen varieties of pelts were on display. Not one was worth a second glance. Some were too coarse, some too brittle, some too heavy. All gave off an unpleasant odor that clung tenaciously to the wearer. Dunan cared nothing for the pelts, although he concealed his disinterest. He knew what he wanted.

Seb Dunan had never seen a gorwol pelt, but he knew the description by heart. A silvery-white so pale it seemed to glow with its own inner light. So soft it could be crushed to wafer thinness by the firm pressure of a hand, so resilient it sprang back to fullness in an instant without a trace of impress. As light as breath, yet warmer than a triple thickness of any other known material and durable as the timeless ruins of Dumabb-Paraxx. Always rare, now considered unobtainable, gorwol pelts would soon be priceless. He had to find a source.

He moved from one mound of furs to another, to outward appearances casual, slightly bored, a man passing time idly. But as he brushed his finger tips over one pelt, lifted another to the light, sniffed gingerly at a third, his eyes went everywhere in search of the smoky fur of the gorwol. He saw no trace of it. A gruff voice startled him.

"Heading up the Moharil? You'll need warm robes for that," the merchant said. He tugged loose a dark, shaggy pelt, and with visible effort, lifted it for Dunan's inspection.

"Too heavy for me," Dunan said.

"It will keep you warm and dry. Feel it," the merchant persisted.

Dunan thrust his hand into the thick fur to the fleecy undercoat. "The outer fur is too coarse. It feels like needles."

"You'll soon get used to it. Tormagon fur is the best you can get these days."

"Tormagon?" Dunan was taken aback. "I thought tormagons were semihuman." He withdrew his hand quickly.

"They're animals, traveler. Good for fur, that's all."

"But aren't they intelligent?"

The Hraggellian cocked an ear scornfully. "Not this one. It was caught, wasn't it?"

Dunan was uncertain whether he was experiencing a rude attempt at humor, Hraggellian style, or simple insensitivity. The merchant's expression revealed nothing, and the latter possibility seemed the more likely. A plain blunt man; very well, then, we'll have plain blunt words, Dunan thought, and came directly to the point.

"I'm looking for gorwol pelts," he said.

"You'll have no more luck than Daldirian in his quest for the fiery crown. None to be had. What are you, a free trader?"

"I used to be. I work with a trading league now. We can pay a good price, and we'll take all you can provide."

"Too late. I haven't even seen a gorwol pelt in twelve darks. Someone brought a few into Norion two darks ago. Sold them to a combine of free traders," the merchant said.

Dunan asked the reported price. He knew that rumor would inflate the figure, but even so, he was startled. Converted into intersystemic currency, it represented the cost of a small fleet of driveships. He blinked rapidly and asked, "All that—for four gorwol skins, you say?"

"Very special skins, trader—the last ones on Hraggellon."

"Are you sure of that? What happened to the gorwol, anyway? They've always been rare, but there was never any talk of their dying out. How could it happen so suddenly?"

"It's not just the gorwol dying out. The Onhla, too." The merchant twitched an ear, looked around cautiously, and drew Seb Dunan closer. "Onhla were the only ones could hunt the gorwol, and they're all gone. Plague. The furs I told you about—they were taken from the corpse of the last Onhla on this planet. I heard that from someone who was there and saw it with his own eyes."

"Aren't there some Onhla living in Norion?"

"Crossbreeds," the merchant said, scratching himself and looking contemptuous at the thought of them. "They're outcasts. Wouldn't dare to set foot on tribal ground. They're rotten hunters, anyway. Gone soft."

"All right, then: suppose the Onhla are all dead. Isn't there anyone else who knows how to track gorwol?"

The merchant frowned. "No. What good would it do? The gorwol are gone, too."

"How can anyone be sure?" Dunan asked.

"We know," the merchant said flatly. "It makes sense. They kept retreating farther and farther into Starside to escape the hunters. Finally they went so deep that nobody but an Onhla could go after them and survive. But over in Starside there are places so cold that even gorwol can't endure. They had to stop. The Onhla caught up to them and killed them all. Then the plague struck down the Onhla." He looked at Dunan, smug and satisfied with his display of logic.

"Has anyone tried to find a surviving Onhla?" Dunan asked.

The merchant looked at him with dawning suspicion. "Why? We know they're all dead."

There was clearly nothing more to be learned from this fellow or his neighbors. Their minds were as impenetrable as the dome of their settlement. They could not conceive of adaptation—and that in itself was absurd, considering how they had adapted to a world part eternal night and cold and darkness, part unending sunlight and parched waste, and the rest enduring a year-long cycle of day and night. The folk of Norion assumed simple reactions, simple solutions to everything, clear-cut answers that required no thinking. No more gorwol pelts coming into market? Then the gorwol and its hunters were dead. Simple as that. The idiots, Dunan thought contemptuously. Grief to the lot of them.

He got away as soon as he could—one had to be polite in this business, even with idiots—and headed back the way he came. This could be bad news, but he was not ready to accept it. He could not let himself believe it. If no gorwol furs were to be had on Hraggellon, he was in serious trouble.

Life had not been like this when he was a free trader. He

walked on slowly, remembering the old times. Good times, they were. The risks were always high, but the rewards were great. How many round trips have I made between wealth and poverty? He did not trouble to compute the answer. It was many, he knew.

Never had to take on anyone I didn't like, not then. The free traders were always the freest starfarers in the galaxy. Not many left now, he thought glumly. The whole galaxy's getting too organized, too big, impersonal. Have to join up to get along now. Sometimes a man doesn't have much choice.

He recalled his own decision, if that word could properly be applied in his case. Doing well on an isolated world, and then the white ship landed. The Sternverein had come to trade. But Seb Dunan did all the trading still, for he was trusted while the somber newcomers were feared. Then came their ultimatum: co-operate with the Sternverein or we can't be responsible for your safety among these barbarians. It was delivered, tersely, in the captain's quarters of the white ship. A lot of armed men around; none of them the friends of Seb Dunan. He understood who the barbarians were, but he was a trader, not a hero. And even a trained warrior could not stand up to the Sternverein. No one could.

And so he joined, and now he sought out likely trade goods for the Sternverein. Best thing, probably. Too old to be caroming from system to system, dodging pirates, slavers, local tyrants, and all the competitors. The Sternverein wasn't all that bad. Certainly did protect members against outside force. Had to give them that.

But the Sternverein did not accept failure. And his mission on Hraggellon was to acquire gorwol pelts and other luxuries; for luxuries were the only items valuable enough to justify the cost of intersystemic trade. The light-globes and the clingers would do for "others"; but there was no getting around the express command to get gorwol pelts. Could be trouble in store, if that merchant had told the truth. Could be a lot of trouble, all Seb Dunan's. The Sternverein did not listen to excuses.

He felt the chill of the air, and looked around him for a source of warmth. Like to watch a smoke-spinner, he thought, but it's too cold to stand watching anything, or listening to a reciter. These people stand and listen to tales of their Daldirian until you'd think their blood would freeze. Grief to them all.

He was almost back to his caravansary by this time, so he hurried on. There was a warming room on the first level, with two huge fires constantly burning. Just what he wanted.

He settled cautiously on the slab bench before the fire, opening his robe to the welcome heat. Over the fireplace hung a tulk's head, bristling with sharp horns, scowling defiantly at all below. Ugly creature, Dunan thought. Just right for an ugly world. He and Hraggellon deserve each other.

Dunan turned his attention elsewhere. The warming room was well occupied, though few of the others were as interested in the fire as he. The natives used the room for social purposes as much as for warming. They had their own way of fighting the cold. They sat in twos and threes, drinking the potent milky Hraggellian liquor. They were a glum and silent lot. This was not, Dunan decided, a planet of carousers; not during darktime, at any rate.

So far, he had seen no victims of memur, the spell-like violence that came suddenly upon dwellers in Norion in the depth of darktime. He had no desire for the sight. From all he had heard, memur was as dangerous for the onlookers as for the victim. No wonder they crack, he thought. Wind and gloom and the stink of people and beasts huddled in this dreary cave of a place. Big as it is, it's still a cave. Can't blame them for exploding. Just hope no one decides to go memur here and now.

Directly behind him, three men were discussing their new regime in guarded voices. Off in a corner, four merchants were working out an elaborate contract while two Remembrancers stood by in witness. The fringe on their robes identified them as lildodes, Truespeakers, members of one of the lower orders of Remembrancers. Dunan recognized them as minors merely from seeing their work. The great ones among the Remembrancers did not earn their keep by memorizing business transactions. Still, someone had to do it if the Hraggellian economy was to thrive.

Odd, the way a race creates a problem, then creates a solution for it, and then congratulates itself on its progress, he reflected. Hraggellon has no written language and wants none. Some ancient prohibition, apparently. So an entire tribe of people become recorders of their civilization. Amazing. Nothing like that on the other worlds I've seen.

Soundscribers: that's what these people would want most, he judged, instinctively touching the one that hung around his neck. Small, perfectly accurate, completely reliable. Machines don't forget. Although everyone claims the Remembrancers don't, either. Worth considering, though. But what would they offer in exchange? Don't need memories, I need gorwol pelts. I won't get them from Remembrancers.

He looked around, covertly studying the company, and his gaze came to rest for a moment on the entry and the figure therein framed. He ducked his head at once, and hoped he had not been seen. The last person on Hraggellon he wanted to see now—or ever—was his assistant. Grief to him for coming here now!

But it was too late to escape. Clell had seen him, and now he strode forward to join him on the bench. The young man walked with the gait of a conqueror and returned disdainful glances to the curious stares drawn by his attire. Clell Basedow, mere apprentice to a trader, dressed like a Grand Commodore of the Sternverein and bore himself like an emperor. Unfortunately, he was a fool.

No one would have taken this strutting fop on a mission by choice. Seb Dunan had always worked with carefully chosen hands, or else done the job alone. But the Basedows were a powerful Sternverein family. What Clell demanded, he always got. It never satisfied him, but that was the Sternverein's problem, not Dunan's. Not until this trip.

Dunan sighed and made room on the bench. No more Onhla, no more gorwol, and now the company of Clell. What a way to begin a mission, he thought despondently.

Clell swirled his black-and-silver cape wide and seated himself by the old trader's side. The fire gleamed on his braid and buttons and highly polished boots. He was fit adornment for a Trulban court ceremony, Dunan thought, but ludicrously out of place here.

"Where did you go? I wanted to talk to you, and you were gone," Clell greeted him. He avoided Hraggellian and voiced his complaints imperiously in the starfarer's common tongue.

"I'm here to work. I was looking the place over, seeing what's available and what's needed."

"Did you go among the people dressed like that?" Clell asked with distaste. "We represent the Sternverein. You should show it in your dress. Impress these brutes."

"I'll leave that to you. I'm comfortable in my old robes."

"Why didn't you take me with you? You're supposed to be instructing me."

"I'll take you with me when the time comes. First I want to familiarize myself with the situation. A lot of things have changed since the Fifth mission team delivered their report."

"The climate has certainly changed. Where's all the ice I heard about? It's cold enough, but I haven't seen much ice."

"If you want to see ice, go to Starside," Dunan suggested. He wished fervently that Clell would take his advice and depart forthwith, to remain absent forever.

"I *don't* want to see ice. The galaxy is full of planets covered with ice," the young man said petulantly.

"Have it your way. Don't go to Starside," Dunan said.

"How long are we going to stay in this wretched, stinking Norion? We'll never get the smell out of our clothing."

"We just arrived. Be patient."

"I want to start hunting. Have you found out where the gorwol are? Do you know what we'll need?" Clell asked.

He was coming too close to the topic Dunan wished to avoid. Something had to be done. Drastic measures, however attractive they might appear, were out of the question. Dunan was accountable for the boy's safety. But there were other ways.

"Stop worrying so much, Clell. Let's have something to warm us up," he said cordially.

Clell was wary. "Whatever they serve here must be poisonous."

"Third Contact okayed planetary food and drink. Just a thurt or two, and we'll drink them slowly. To warm the blood. It's part of your training."

"Training?"

"Of course. When I was working the Skeggjatt System, all the trading took place at the inns. Nearly ruined my insides, but I made the trades. Come on, Clell. It's time you started learning," Dunan said, signaling for the thurt-boy and holding up two fingers.

A thurt was an amount of liquid equal to what a grown man could hold in his cupped hands without spillage. It was, understandably, a flexible measure, but even a stingy thurt of Hraggellian liquor was damaging to a novice. Three were incapacitating. Dunan, who knew the proper protective measures, decided that he would treat Clell to three. That would buy the time to make inquiries without interference from his assistant.

Clell's disposition did not change with a single thurt. He merely complained louder, and in greater detail, slurring his words slightly. Dunan was grateful for the youth's failure to master Hraggellian. He was saying things about Norion that men do not allow to be said about their homes with impunity. Only the fact that he was saying them in an unknown tongue saved them from an unpleasant scene.

Clell jabbered on, into his second thurt, and Dunan's attention wandered. He found himself eavesdropping on the three plotters who sat at his back. Hearing his unfamiliar speech, they had grown less guarded. Their voices were audible, when Clell's inventory of complaints did not drown out all other sound.

The three were not happy under the rule of Orm the Peacebringer. Their mildest epithet for him was "Orm the Usurper." Dunan became interested and listened as carefully as he could without arousing their suspicion. The new regime had come into power since the departure of the previous Sternverein representatives on Hraggellon, so Dunan had learned of it only after arrival. Orm and his followers were a secretive bunch, and Dunan was glad for whatever information he could acquire.

Even when he allowed for the distortion of disgruntled opponents, the picture of Norion's new ruler was a forbidding one. Cruel deeds had been done in the long famine and the plagues that followed it, but Orm's cruelty had exceeded all others'. He had betrayed his allies one by one, turned his enemies against one another, and then sided with the stronger to destroy the weaker even as he plotted to betray the victor. He had killed without regard for ancestral, tribal, or memorial law. Now, having seized the rule of Norion by murder and treachery, he was methodically eliminating all opponents and potential rivals. Or so one of the speakers charged, and was free with details.

Orm's personal assassins, the Sixty Without Names, seemed able to be everywhere at once. Hundreds had died mysteriously at their hands. Surely, some greater power was behind all this, the speaker hinted. One need only consider the events of recent times: a few darks ago, when the plague ended, Orm was a placeless schemer from one of the minor families, without even Remembrancers of his own. And now he was ruler, and his position grew stronger with each passing dark.

The others expressed doubt, but the speaker persisted. A loner like Orm could not have come this far without some new and powerful backing. His rise had been too sudden, too smooth.

The discussion ended with that question unresolved. As the three made their way by him, Dunan stole a quick covert glance. They passed too quickly for him to distinguish faces, but he noticed the clumsily patched tormagon robe worn by the one who had done most of the talking. The others wore nondescript robes of blackish-brown fur, very ripe and odorous. Dunan sought the relief of his scent-case.

By now, Clell was nodding. His speech was hesitant. Two empty thurts stood on the floor near his gleaming boots. Another would not be necessary. Clell would sleep long and soundly and be disinclined to activity for some time after waking.

Dunan placed his own thurt, brimming and untouched, on the floor, and began to haul his young assistant to his feet. Their rooms were three ramps up and on the opposite wing, just beyond the windward curve. It would not be easy, guiding a husky fellow like Clell all that way, along these narrow galleries. But Dunan did not begrudge the effort. He had bought himself an interval of peace and quiet.

They left the warming room and made their way past the dark piles of goods stored here in the open center of the caravansary. High above, on the underside of the dome, light-globes burned at irregular intervals, throwing just enough light to enable them to pick their way to the first ramp.

Dunan was wary and alert. Hraggellian tradition condemned any attack upon a stranger, but traditions were often broken. He felt uneasy in this isolated place of shadows and darkness. When he looked up and saw a great flapping shape descending to land with a dull thump almost at his feet, he gave a cry and jumped back. Clell was in the way, and the two of them went down. Dunan struggled to his feet and set his back to a heap of goods. The fallen thing lay without moving. It made no sound. Clell moaned, tried to rise, and then abandoned himself to sleep. The other still lay unmoving.

Dunan stepped forward cautiously. Others were coming now, roused by his outcry. He knelt beside the crumpled figure on the ground, and in the light of the thurt-boy's globe he saw a clumsily patched tormagon robe.

"That's Osmidap, isn't it? How'd he get here?"

"Fell. I saw him fall. From the top ramp."

"Dead as the stone knights of Hrull. His back is broken."

"What was he doing up there?"

"Where are the two strangers he was with?"

"Memur got them. One of them went memur."

"No. We would have heard him screaming."

The questions came all at once, in a flurry, and then they stopped abruptly. No more was said. The answer to all the questions was unmistakably clear. The dead man himself had said it: the Sixty Without Names were everywhere at once.

Sympathetic Hraggellians helped Seb Dunan haul his snoring assistant to his quarters. Safely within his own chamber, Dunan mulled over what he had seen and heard. There had been no trouble so far, not even a hint of it. The rulers had given no indication that they were even aware of his presence on Hraggellon. But that could change in an instant. Even now, he might be in danger merely from having chanced to overhear what he had, and seen the body fall. It would be best to transact his business quickly and be off this world as soon as possible.

The first necessity was to find an Onhla tribesman.

. . . that sometime between 2650 and 2710 GSC an unaffiliated driveship transported a group of Onhla to another world. There are some indications that the world was Insgar. The number taken is uncertain. Some accounts say fewer than a dozen, others a full tribe.

The Remembrancer who gave the most detailed account spoke of a red ship with a crew of tall, brown-skinned, white-haired humans. All accounts stress the willingness of the Onhla to make the voyage. This, and the description of the ship and its crew, effectively rule out a slaver raid.

Description of the crew accords with no race known at present; we therefore consider. . . .

Eno Glaser, Tertiary

Second Hraggellon Contact Mission

III.

THE MEETING

Hraggellon's sun appeared on the horizon and began its slow ascent. The shadow line withdrew ever more deeply into Starside. Over Norion, the skies grew steadily brighter. The drone of the pundergorn dwindled and died, and the first breath of the day wind, the gentle galendergorn, caressed the city. Another dark was past, and the land around Norion came to life. The age-old cycle continued. Upriver with the light, downriver to Norion as the darktime drew near. Plant and reap and rest; plant and reap and take shelter until another darktime; then begin again.

It was a busy time. The huge Brightside shutters were hauled back, and the narrow Starside windslits were opened to allow the galendergorn to carry its freshness and warmth through the city. The first planting was begun while the ground was still in thaw; first harvest had to be in before the full heat of midlight baked the ground and withered all growing things. The ice began to break in the Moharil valley. Life-giving waters coursed to the fields, and the rivercraft were made ready for their journeys.

With the return of light, the sullen populace of Norion seemed to change. They moved more briskly, slept less, ate more, worked harder. Even Seb Dunan, unaccustomed to the living patterns of a planet with a year-long day, found himself stimulated. When his weary body said "sleep" his senses said "work" and kept him active beyond his own expectations of endurance. When his energy flagged, the scent-case carried him through.

He needed all the time and energy he could summon. Norion had a darktime population of over a hundred thousand inhabitants, any one of whom might have information about the Onhla. Considering the political situation, Dunan felt it wisest to conduct his inquiry by himself. It was a safer method, but painfully slow. He had not been able to speak with more than a tiny fraction of the townspeople in the waning darktime, and now, with the return of light, half the population were ready to depart. Few could spare time for an old trader's questions.

If there were any Onhla in Norion, they would almost certainly be leaving, heading upriver, following the shadow line. Onhla could easily adapt to the heat of midlight, even on the fringe of the Brightside desert, but they preferred the cold and darkness of Starside, their ancestral hunting grounds.

Onhla seemed capable of adapting to any climate. Indeed, their physical plasticity was such that the Sternverein contact teams had long been uncertain whether they were members of one species or of many. Not only did they adapt to suit the surrounding climate, they also changed form as they aged.

It was known that in youth and adolescence, they were physically close to animals. Many young Onhla ran with their tribe's tormagon packs. With the onset of sexual maturity, they assumed a nearly human appearance, which they retained throughout their long life. What happened to them in old age was uncertain. Most likely, they died—or entered the long dream, as they described it. But there were vague tales of a third life-phase, a time of renewed physical growth and altered mental powers that came rarely and unpredictably to a mature Onhla. These elders were said to lose the ability, or the desire, to adapt to climatic change. They remained deep in Starside, beyond all human observers. Convenient for them, Dunan thought. Probably a primitive way of explaining why no one has ever seen one. Nonsense, all of it, surely.

The Onhla were a strange race; strange enough to make Seb Dunan uneasy at the thought of dealing with them. He had done business of one kind or another with a score of humanoid races, but not one of the others had seemed to him to exhibit such total alienness. The Onhla, after all, talked with animals. There were even people in Norion who swore that the elder Onhla of Starside (whom they had never seen) bore tails.

But as Dunan repeatedly told himself, Onhla help was necessary if he was to succeed. He did not have to like them, or feel easy among them. He had only to find them— find one of them, only one—and get him to work taking gorwol pelts. Simple enough, really, once he found the creature.

That was his sole task now, and it consumed all his waking time. He walked the arcades and galleries of Norion, visiting every level of the city, questioning every pelt merchant, every new acquaintance, and hearing always the same story. The gorwol is extinct as Abapp and the ancient race of dwarfs. The Onhla are all dead. And still he searched, and Clell complained ever more loudly, and the townspeople of Norion worked on under the lengthening light.

The galendergorn grew steadily warmer. The first green shoots burst up in the lowland planting fields. The bankside quays swarmed with miners and planters eager to get upriver and set to work. Seb Dunan, exhausted and disappointed, dragged himself to an inn near Norion's Starside portal. Time no longer had a meaning for him. He knew only that he was hungry and aching with fatigue, and must sleep a long sleep soon if he was to continue his search.

He ordered the first item to catch his eye. The skeep and gauntlings were delicious, fresh-caught from the rushing river, but he had little appetite. He ate what he could, forced himself to rise, and left by the path that passed the stable. But at his first glimpse of the stablekeeper, all his weariness dropped away.

Nothing was certain at a single look, of course, but the fellow had the Onhla stature and bulk. Dunan seated himself on the outdoor bench, in the sun, and studied him. His

skin was reddening, but it had a smooth waxen look to it—
and that was characteristic of the mature Onhla. His nose
was flattened, his eyes sunk deep under a sheltering brow
ridge. Thick brown hair, barred with gold, covered his head
and hung down his back almost to the waist.

He showed the signs of an Onhla. He could be a true
Onhla, perhaps the last one on Hraggellon. Seb Dunan felt
his heart beat faster, and he forced himself to sit still for a
time. He brought the scent-case to his nostrils and breathed
deeply, calming himself. Foolish to get your hopes up, he
told himself. This could be a crossbreed like all the others,
worse than useless. For an Onhla to mate with any but another Onhla was the ultimate disgrace. The child of such a
union might look like an Onhla, but would know—or wish to
know—none of the tribal ways. It would have the weaknesses
of both parents and the strength of neither.

Dunan took a deep, calming breath, snapped shut the
scent-case, and rose to approach the stablekeeper. As Dunan
drew closer, the reek of the stables became almost unbeara-
ble. They were crowded at this season, and there was no
time to spare for cleanliness. Dunan opened the scent-case
once again and kept his hand near his face.

The stablekeeper turned as Dunan approached, and stood
before him like a column. "What do you want?" the fellow
demanded in an expressionless voice.

"I want to speak with you," Dunan replied.

"A stablekeeper does not talk, he works. I have much
work to do."

"I believe you're an Onhla tribesman. If you are, I can
offer you more suitable work," Dunan said bluntly.

The stablekeeper was silent for a time, with his steady
gaze on the old trader. Finally he said, "All the Onhla are
dead. Everyone in Norion says this."

"I've heard it said often. I don't believe it."

"What work is more suitable for an Onhla than the work I
do here?"

"Hunting."

The big creature was silent, standing motionless before him. After a time, he replied, "The Onhla are dead, slain by the falling sickness. Go away." Then he turned, and without a backward look, entered the stables.

There was nothing more to say, nothing to do. Dunan had no wish to linger in the miasma of the stables, so he took his leave at once. His sleeping chamber was halfway across Norion, and he wished he could be there at once. This had been a blow. This time he was sure he had found his hunter, but it was just another surly crossbreed. Grief to him. Grief to them all, and to this filthy planet, he thought. His heart sank, and in his weariness he felt close to despair. He was scarcely aware of the long walk through the busy arcade.

He dropped on his sleeping platform, robe, boots, and all, and slept a long exhausted sleep. When he awoke, the stable-keeper was in his chamber, squatting against the outer wall, opposite him. Dunan propped himself up, blinking, much confused.

"What are you doing here? How did you get in?" he demanded.

His questions were ignored. The big man, without stirring, said, "You spoke of work for an Onhla. Say more."

Seb Dunan plunged ahead. "I want gorwol furs, and no one but an Onhla can take them. If you are truly an Onhla— and now I believe you are—you know you were born to hunt, not to serve. Bring me gorwol furs and I'll pay you a good price."

"In Norion, they all say that the last gorwol died long ago and they are now extinct."

Dunan gave a gesture of dismissal and said, "They also say the Onhla are dead. I believe very little that I hear in Norion. Do you accept my offer?"

Again the stablekeeper held a lengthy silence; finally he replied, "I will leave you for a time. Sleep again, and then come to the inn for your answer."

Seb Dunan did just that. He rose and ate and spent much time making plans and being very content with himself, and then he settled down for his best sleep since arrival on Hraggellon.

Clell insisted on accompanying him to the inn, and Dunan agreed reluctantly, only after issuing solemn orders to his assistant to remain silent while any agreement was made. However exalted Clell Basedow's connections might be, he was still only an apprentice, and not a very promising one. Seb Dunan was accountable for this mission, and he meant to run it his way.

Clell accepted the condition of silence, considering it a modest price for the learning experience. He eased his burden by keeping up a steady recitation of complaints about the food, the noise, the crowds, the heat, and the stench of Norion. Dunan bore it patiently, sustained by the thought of his assistant breathing deeply of the rich stable aroma.

The stablekeeper was waiting by the entrance. He was still filthy, still dressed in the rags he had worn when Dunan last saw him, but he seemed somehow different. On his shoulder he carried a small bundle. His greeting was direct.

"Agree to my price and I will hunt for you," he said.

"Tell me the price."

"Take me to Insgar and bring me back again, along with those I take from Insgar."

Dunan frowned thoughtfully. "Insgar is a long way from here. Do you know anything about intersystemic flight? Have you ever been in space?"

"Take me to Insgar," the other said, ignoring the questions. "That is the price of my hunting."

"And what do I get? How many gorwol skins?"

The stablekeeper extended four fingers of his hand. "As many as these," he said.

Dunan waved that off. "Not enough. This many," he said, extending both hands, fingers spread wide.

"Not that many gorwol can be taken."

Dunan turned back two fingers, then another, and then one more. He held at six. "It must be this many."

The Onhla again extended one hand, then held the thumb of the other hand beside it. "This many. I agree."

"Good. I'll get a Truespeaker, and we can repeat—" Seb Dunan began, but the Onhla broke in, "We need no Remembrancer. We are not townspeople. The agreement is made, and we must honor it."

"That's all right with me. When do you want to leave?"

"Now," the Onhla said.

He started for the riverbank, and they followed close behind. Clell walked by Seb Dunan's side, looking displeased and slightly ill. His boots—new ones—were smeared with stable muck and he repeatedly wrinkled his nose in disgust.

"If you don't like bad smells, you ought to get yourself a scent-case," Dunan said pleasantly.

"I don't believe in those otherworlder poisons," was Clell's flat reply.

"Not a poison. Just a mild stimulant with a pleasant odor. Everyone uses them on Tarquin."

Clell's voice was bitter. "Oh yes, just a mild stimulant. Like the poison you had me drink when we arrived. I was a long time recovering from that."

"So I noticed. Too bad. You'll have to learn to handle worse than that if you intend to make a life in the Sternverein."

"Right now I'm wondering how to handle your new friend. Do you really intend to go chasing off to Insgar and back?"

Seb Dunan looked at his assistant disapprovingly. "Of course I do. That's the agreement."

"But what can he do if you simply take the gorwol furs and leave Hraggellon? You have the Sternverein behind you, and he's only one semihuman creature on a minor world."

"We made an agreement," Dunan repeated, saying the words slowly and distinctly.

Basedow laughed. "No Remembrancer witnessed it. The Onhla can't claim enforcement. I think it's foolish to waste a long voyage—"

"Be quiet, Clell," Dunan cut in. "I don't care what you think. If you learn nothing more from me, learn that a trader keeps his word. Learn it and never forget it."

Clell sulked for a time. They were drawing closer to the quays now. The Onhla strode on, a dozen paces ahead, his step steady and purposeful. He did not once look back.

Abruptly, Clell demanded, "Why would he want to go to Insgar? It's no better than Hraggellon, from what I hear."

"I think I know why. I'll have to check the ship's information center for specifics, but I remember hearing of a group of Onhla being brought to Insgar long ago. When he realized that the rest of his race were dead, this fellow must have remembered stories of the Onhla on Insgar. They're his only hope of restoring his tribe. Without them, he'll be the last Onhla on this world."

"So we're to be interplanetary marriage-makers."

"We're to do what we agreed to do, provided he delivers the pelts. We'll take him to Insgar, and then bring him and whoever he finds there back to Hraggellon," Dunan said. "For my part, I hope he finds a whole tribe. If the Onhla are restored, and we have the exclusive right to trade with them, we can do very well. Even the Sternverein will be impressed by that."

They proceeded in silence. Just before they reached the quays, the Onhla turned down a pathway that led upriver. He walked as one on familiar ground. Seb Dunan followed, and Clell remained close at hand.

The path ended in a clearing on the bank of the Moharil. The river was high, and the current strong. The Onhla walked to the water's edge, then turned to face the two traders. He tossed his bundle to the ground at Seb Dunan's feet with the command, "Guard this," and then he began to strip off his filthy garments and fling them away.

"What are you doing?" Clell asked uneasily.

The Onhla made no reply. From a nearby bush, he pulled the smallest leaves and rubbed them into his skin, meanwhile walking to the river's edge.

"Don't! The current will sweep you to your death. That water's ice cold!" Dunan cried, lunging forward.

The Onhla swiveled his head and stared at the old trader, stopping him in his tracks. Then, with a cry that drowned out the roaring of the river, he flung himself into the dark water. Seb Dunan and Clell rushed to the bank, but saw no sign of him. Swollen by the melted ice that coursed through the open floodgates of Lake Kariar, the river Moharil swept past only a hand's breadth below the crest of the bank.

"He's killed himself," Clell said in a numb voice. "No one could live in this water."

"An Onhla could. If he comes out, we'll know we've got the right man."

"If he doesn't, we're in trouble. We were seen leaving the inn with him. We might have been followed."

"I doubt it. If he doesn't come back, we'll toss his bundle into the river and drink a thurt to his memory." Dunan sighed and turned to his assistant. "Sit down, make yourself comfortable. I want to wait until I'm sure."

Clell remained standing, and used the interval to clean his boots. Seb Dunan sat with his eyes fixed on the roiling waters. At last the Onhla's head and shoulders burst from the river in a shower of spray, then plunged beneath the surface once again. Dunan noted, with astonishment, that he had reappeared upstream from where he had entered. He had heard stories of Onhla strength, but not believed them. Now he believed. Anything that could make headway against this current was as strong as a Quespodon. He began to feel much encouraged.

"So you've found your tribesman," Clell said.

"I certainly have. Maybe the last one on Hraggellon, and he works for me, now. If there's a gorwol left, he'll find it."

"It all seems so simple, really."

Dunan turned and looked incredulously at his assistant. "Simple? Grief to you, boy, what do you mean, *simple!* I walked from one end of Norion to the other, up and down every ramp in the place, poked into every stinking corner . . . it was not simple, Clell, not simple at all. It may have seemed so to you, but only because you did nothing but polish your boots while I walked on mine."

"I know you worked hard. I would have helped, but you never took me along. You did everything by yourself," Clell sulked.

"Half the time you were off on some business of your own. Besides, that's my way. I've been a loner too long to change. Let's forget it. But I want you to know that it was not a simple job, my boy."

Clell was slightly mollified. "I only meant that all it took was hard work. The Onhla was right here in Norion, where anyone could have found him if they really tried. Why didn't any of the fur merchants think of doing what you did?" he asked.

"Hraggellians don't think that way. They believe what they're told. They heard that the Onhla were dead, and it never occurred to any of them to question it. If any of them saw this fellow, they assumed he was a crossbreed."

"What a pack of idiots," Clell said.

"Not exactly. They just think differently from us. Maybe it's an effect of the climate." When Clell looked puzzled, Seb Dunan explained, "The Hraggellians accept what they know is sure to come, and life goes on smoothly. The wind shifts, the river rises, the crops grow, all on schedule. The weather on this world is rotten, I agree, but it's *predictably* rotten. They always know what's coming next, so they feel no urge to ask questions—not about the climate, not about anything. Maybe they *are* idiots. I don't know. They seem happy enough."

Seb Dunan fell silent. He saw the Onhla surface once again, farther upstream than before. The creature's strength was amazing. He bobbed up once more to fix his bearings, then began to swim to where the two traders waited.

Clell had not noticed; perhaps he saw and did not care. "If they're so trusting, why do they need the Remembrancers? Your Onhla didn't want to use them."

Dunan replied without turning, his eyes fixed on the figure cutting steadily through the water to them. "Trusting and remembering are different things. If two people make an agreement, both might forget the details in ten darks' time. Or they might both die, and someone else would have to figure out what they had agreed. The Remembrancers are necessary."

"Some people don't think so," Clell said cryptically.

"Then they don't have to. Come on, let's give this fellow a hand ashore."

They stood at the bank, ready to assist the Onhla, but their help was not required. He scrambled to dry ground, gestured them off, then shook himself as an animal does. With the ease of familiarity, he tore larger leaves from the low bush near at hand and used them to blot himself dry. Then he plucked pale green berries from the same bush, crushed them between his palms, and smeared the juice over his body and through his hair. The clear fluid gave off a sharp, pleasant smell.

Dunan, curious, picked a few berries, squeezed them, and rubbed the juice on the back of his hand. It caused a tingling, cooling sensation.

"What do you call this?" he asked the Onhla.

"Rendrood, the purifier," the tribesman replied, reaching for more berries. "We clean and dry and scent our skins with it. Prepare the berries properly and they will purge many inner pains. It is a useful plant."

"It certainly is," Dunan agreed. He broke off a branch heavily laden with berries and plucked a leaf from below them. Good trade items, he thought.

The Onhla squatted to undo his bundle, the great humped muscles of his back bulging as he worked. The bundle held only a few simple articles of clothing, which he proceeded to don. Over his short sleeveless undergarment of soft leather scraped to almost transparent thinness, he tied a loose, vestlike arrangement of knotted strips of leather. Neither of the traders had ever seen such a garment—if garment it was—and Clell's curiosity got the better of him.

"What's that?" he asked.

"The history of the tribe of Bachan, such as I remember."

"Those knots are a kind of writing, then."

"Writing?"

Clell looked at him hopelessly. Dunan recalled that the very concept of writing was unknown on this world, and tried to explain. "Writing is a way of recording things that have been done and said, so that others, who were not present at the doing and the saying, can know of them. It's like what the Remembrancers do with their memories," he said.

The tribesman weighed this as he put on his outer garment, a brown tunic with a broad gold stripe, the colors of the Bachan. At length, he said, "True, they are writing. They allow words and deeds to live on beyond the saying and the doing."

"What do the knots tell?" Dunan asked.

"Only another of my tribe may know," said the Onhla. He stooped to remove the last items from the pile, two broad daggers of a yellowed ivorylike substance, each about the length of his forearm. Dunan asked to inspect one, and the tribesman handed it to him. The trader inspected it closely as the Onhla wrapped the other around his wrist and fixed it in place.

"Made of some kind of bone, isn't it?" Dunan asked.

"The inner ribs of the gorwol."

"It's flexible. Is it strong?"

The Onhla said nothing. He stepped into the low growth by the clearing, selected a stalk about the thickness of his wrist, and gestured the others closer. Pointing to the stalk, he said, "Cut this with your blade."

Dunan observed the thickness of the stalk and said, "Give it a try, Clell. You're the strong one."

Basedow flung back his cloak, drew his dagger, and set himself before the stalk. With a mighty slash, he buried the blade about one third of the way into it. He had a bit of difficulty wrenching loose.

Hult stepped forward. He held out his hand, and Dunan returned the yellow blade to him. With four casual strokes, he lopped off the top of the stalk and cut three even slices from below it. Picking up the slices, he gave one to each of the traders and took one for himself.

"Chew," he said as he wound the blade around his other wrist. "The taste is pleasant and it will give you strength."

Dunan slipped the piece into his pocket, along with the samples of rendrood. The Onhla was proving a useful fellow. "I'll try it later," he said. "Come into Norion with us now, and we'll pick up your supplies."

"I need no supplies."

"But you can't just go into Starside without . . ." Dunan blurted, and then checked himself. "No, maybe you can. But we can't. We'll need clothing and food."

"You need nothing. You will not come. I hunt alone."

"We'll only go part of the way. We want to help you. We're partners now."

"You cannot help. Even I cannot survive long in the part of Starside where the gorwol dwell. Our sun never shines there. You would die long before we reached it. You need only buy me a passage upriver, and tell me where we will meet at the coming of the next dark."

Clell tugged at his sleeve, but Dunan shook the hand off and said, "Agreed. Can you suggest a place?"

"At your ship."

Dunan thought about that for a moment and found it to his liking. Meeting the Onhla at the ship left the least time for anyone to learn what he was up to. He began to give directions, but the tribesman cut him short.

"I know where your ship is," he said.

Dunan gave him a hard, appraising look. "I'm beginning to think you were looking for me as hard as I was looking for you. That trip to Insgar must mean a lot to you."

"It was our agreement."

"It was, and I'll keep my part of it. Just bring the gorwol pelts, and you'll get your trip to Insgar and back."

They made their way to the quayside, and the Onhla took a place on a six-sailer bringing a team of miners and a mixed group of planters upriver. His farewell was simple. "I will be at your ship when the floodgates close at darkfall," he said. Then he turned and strode up the gangway without looking back. Only then did Dunan realize that he had never learned the tribesman's name.

He did not allow the oversight to trouble him for more than an instant. He felt too good. He knew he could trust the nameless, taciturn, incredibly strong creature to bring in the pelts that would make Seb Dunan's place in the Sternverein secure for his remaining years.

The bright sails, three to a side, bellied out with the force of the galendergorn, and the slender craft moved smoothly upriver. The traders watched until it disappeared into a crowd of sails, then turned to make their way back along the quay and into the city.

The quay was crowded and noisy, and the traders' path was clogged with bundles in a wide assortment of shapes and sizes, every imaginable color, and as great a variety of aromas as Norion in mid-dark. Dunan had been advised that half Norion's darktime population would be on their way upriver at the return of light, but the sight of this crowd, and the thought of similar crowds at the other points of embarcation, made him wonder if Norion might not become a ghost city in a very short time. Miners, trappers, farmers, and woodcutters were anxious to work lands newly freed from the icy grip of darktime, and most of the workers had families to accompany them. Tools and gear and personal goods were piled everywhere. The inevitable camp-followers and hangers-on were much in evidence. It was a busy, noisy, colorful scene, not unpleasant to the eye of a traveler who has just successfully completed his business and now has a full brighttime at his disposal. Dunan looked about with an approving eye and smiled on the bustling crowds.

"What's his name? Did you get his name?" Clell broke in upon his contentment.

"Whose? The Onhla's, do you mean?"

"Yes, of course. You never mentioned his name."

Dunan thought quickly. "They never tell their names to outsiders. Only another Onhla can be told. And it has to be a member of their own tribe."

"It does?"

"Yes. He showed great trust by revealing that he was of the tribe of Bachan. That was a great gesture of friend-ship," Dunan went on.

Clell looked suspicious. "I never heard of that."

"Well, now you know. That's what you're here for, my boy, to learn. Just listen to me."

They picked their way through the clutter, and came to a place where a solemn group of about forty people were as-sembled, together with their meager possessions. Their robes showed that they were Remembrancers. By the gang-way to a majestic nine-sailer stood two women of high rank, their plain robes richly hung with fringe. They were deep in discussion with the ship's master.

"There's something you won't often see," Dunan informed his assistant, gesturing toward the group. "Remembrancers don't generally travel in large groups like that."

"From what I've been hearing, they may have to change their ways very soon," Clell said with a knowing air.

"Oh? And what have you been hearing, and where? And from whom, if I may ask?"

"I've become acquainted with some people who are very powerful in Orm's regime." He looked to Dunan for approval, and when it was not forthcoming, he quickly, defensively, added, "You always said it was smart to get to know the people in power. I only did what you said a trader ought to do."

"It *is* smart, if you do it right," Dunan said, his heart sinking at the thought of the impression this blowhard must have made on the masters of Norion. "Well, go on—what did they tell you?"

"The Remembrancers are not in Orm's good graces. He believes they wield too much power over the citizens of Norion. After all, they're parasites: they make nothing, produce nothing, and yet they control most of the wealth in the city."

Dunan glanced at the Remembrancers assembled nearby, frowned, and said, "They don't look wealthy to me. Is that all Orm has to say against them?"

"He doesn't accuse them of having the wealth, but of controlling it. They memorize all transactions in Norion, Seb—imagine the havoc they could cause! That's what troubles Orm. He fears for the well-being of his subjects."

"Not much reason to fear. Remembrancers practically worship accuracy. They're not likely to abuse their position."

Clell was not inclined to agree easily. "Even if they don't, there's really no room for them. Orm is bringing a new age to Norion, and the Remembrancers belong to the past. All they do is keep alive the memory of old things. That's all they have in their heads—old things, the past, unimportant things that should have been forgotten long ago. They're boring."

Dunan grunted disapprovingly. Clell was echoing the typical empty speeches of the newly powerful looking for a victim. Dunan himself did not care much about the fate of the Remembrancers; he knew that their way of life was already moribund. As Hraggellon increased its dealings with other worlds, the Remembrancers would prove inadequate to the new complexity of life. Unfortunate, perhaps, but that was the price of progress. Still, he disliked seeing them turned into a handy scapegoat. He had seen tangible proof of Orm's ruthlessness, and the thought of its being directed against this harmless sect disturbed him.

You're getting old, he admonished himself sternly. Worrying about things that are none of your business. The Remembrancers will survive without Seb Dunan's aid. They have until now, anyway. And if they're driven out of Norion, that opens a market for soundscribers. Light-globes and soundscribers. And a few hundred clingers. And those plants the Onhla showed us . . . if they can grow elsewhere . . . have to test that out.

This was going to be a good mission. He felt confident of that now.

Knowledge of the planet is extremely limited, and natives exhibit little curiosity. No oceanic transport of any kind. Offshore currents are unnavigable in any craft known to the Hraggellians. Existence of other land masses generally unsuspected.

No evidence of aerial travel. The planet appears to hold no flying life-forms, and the possibility of flight seems never to have occurred to the natives.

Land vehicles are primitive. Norionites travel on foot within the city enclosure. Haxopods are used chiefly in the colder regions, stabled on the outskirts of Norion in darktime. They are of a strain that cannot tolerate heat.

Commerce and transportation depend on inland waterways. During the period of light, lakes and rivers rise greatly and the wind shifts. The current takes workers downriver, and sail power takes them up the Moharil to Lake Kariar, an immense inland sea. At least five lesser rivers feed into Lake Kariar, and by means of these . . .

Volin Meibon, Secondary

Second Hraggellon Contact Mission

IV.

UPRIVER TO STARSIDE

The Moharil was in full flood now, bringing water to Norion and the fields beyond, filling the reservoirs and holding tanks and cisterns against the long drought of midlight. This early in the lighttime, the galendergorn had not reached its full force, and the trip upriver to the first portage was slow. For most of the passengers, it was also quite uncomfortable.

Hult was not displeased. He found a spot near the prow of the vessel, away from the others, and settled down to rest. He could have walked—even swum—as fast as the boat was moving, but he felt no urgency. He knew how much time his work would require, and he knew that he had that much time, and more. There was no need to hurry. He conserved his strength for the hunt. The cold spray was soothing against his skin, and he slept soundly until they reached the portage.

The roar of falling water obliterated all other sound when he awoke. His boat had pulled into a calm channel behind a breakwater, and when he rose to look around, the deckhands were readying their lines. In moments the boat was made fast, the sails furled, and the first of the passengers were pressing to debark.

The passengers gathered at the assembly point on the bank, there to begin the ascent to Lake Kariar and the second stage of the journey. Each carried his own baggage— one soon learned to travel light on Hraggellon—and the progress up the hillside path was slow. Hult hung back to look over the scene. There was an undeniable grandeur to it, and it pleased him, too, to be able to use the full power of his far-seeing eyes once more. In the confines of the hooded city, he had felt as though things were pressing in upon his vision. But now his sight was unleashed.

The cold water gushed from the floodgates in a foaming arc, thundering in its passage and filling the air with fine spray and mist. As he watched, an empty boat, sails furled, crept from the sanctuary of the breakwater and was instantly seized by the current. It shot forward, irrevocably committed now to the headlong downriver plunge to Norion. There it would take on its next load of eager passengers and begin another slow crawl upriver. Hult watched, breathing deep, relishing the cold, damp air. He had passed two darks within walls, and that was enough. Patience had repaid him well. It was good to be on his way to Starside again.

He caught up to his group, falling in behind two venerable Remembrancers. In his time in the city, he had heard much evil spoken of these people, but he had known them to do none. He found far less evil in them than in those who condemned them.

Those who spoke against the Remembrancers were men much like the young trader. He was clearly not a man to be trusted. The older one seemed honest, but the younger one was like the men of the inns and the ruling chambers. He thought himself better than he was, and would not learn from his mistakes. Such did not last long on Hraggellon. No otherworlder did.

Even the old trader was likely to betray him, given the chance, Hult thought. That was the human way, worst of all among the otherworlders. The humans of Norion were at least sharers of this world, and knew its ways, but otherworlders were a foul lot—a confusion of sizes, shapes, and colors, many harsh tongues, dull senses, foolish traditions, and no truth in them. Their colors meant nothing to them; they wore no histories on their bodies to comfort and strengthen them and to give them identity and significance. They could not endure heat and cold, as the Onhla could. True, they had great ships that moved among the stars at a speed beyond imagining, but they went nowhere of significance. There was nowhere else. Only Hraggellon was fit to live on. The otherworlders rushed from world to world because they were all foolish and greedy. One could work with them, but one must never trust them. Only the Onhla could be trusted.

The pathway was steep, and the elder Remembrancers found it difficult. Each carried a sizable bundle, and they were staggering under their burden. When they stopped to rest a second time, Hult saw that they were near collapse. "I will carry these to the boat," he said to them, taking the bundles from their sides and hoisting them easily to his shoulders.

"We thank you, but we cannot ask a favor," said one.

"You did not ask. I offered," Hult replied.

"But we must . . . we cannot . . ." began the second.

"My strength is greater than yours. Come," Hult said, and walked ahead, ending the discussion. The Remembrancers followed.

Hult was not acting out of goodness. He knew that among the other races of Hraggellon, one grew weaker as time passed, and it annoyed him to see the weak trying to do work the strong should do. Besides, Remembrancers were a good source of information. It was said that they knew everything that had happened on Hraggellon, even in times long past. He would let them repay his strength of body with their strength, the strength of knowledge.

Through his ranging sense, he knew without turning that they were close behind him. He could hear them conversing in low voices. He slowed his pace to allow them to draw nearer, within hearing distance.

The Remembrancers spoke in their own language. Hult had some knowledge of it, but he could not understand all they said. He learned that they were fleeing, seeking refuge. From their intonations he divined the uneasiness of one and the growing fear of the other.

The things he had overheard at the inn were true, then.

Under the new rulers of Norion, resentment for these people was on the rise. These two Remembrancers, and the others traveling with them, sought a safer life at one of the farming settlements on the Upper Moharil, beyond Lake Kariar. Hult saw little hope for them. A few humans lived in those settlements; some lived in even more remote hamlets where much of the year was passed in darkness and bitter cold. Beyond that, in the eternal sunlessness of Starside, none but Onhla could hope to survive.

Remembrancers were dwellers within walls. For too long, they had worked with mind and memory, not with the strength and endurance of their bodies. They were too different from the hard folk who lived in the settlements, and Hult doubted that they could relearn the necessities of survival in time. From the drift of their words, he gathered that they believed a new life was possible. He thought them self-deceived, but said nothing. Onhla never gave advice to outsiders, and seldom offered it to one another. They believed that the important lessons cannot be taught, but must be learned.

They reached the crest. Lake Kariar extended before them in all its immensity, a great inland sea, swollen now to five times its darktime size. Its far end was lost in mist.

The current in the lake was much gentler than the current of the Moharil, and the big flat-bottomed lake craft looked clumsy compared to the narrow sailboats of the river. They were not much more than elaborate rafts, with high masts to catch the last breath of the galendergorn, and nine burly oarsmen to a side.

The boat was nearly loaded, and there was much shouting among passengers and crew. A group of Remembrancers clustered anxiously at the rail, and their relief at the sight of the elders was plain to see. Hult carried the bundles aboard and waited for the old men to join him.

A woman came before him. Her robe bore the leader's heavy fringe. She lightly touched her finger tips to her ear lobe, then to her lips, and then extended her hand before her, palm down, and waited for his reponse. Hult recognized the greeting and returned it. She addressed him in the common dialect of Norion.

"We thank you for your help to our evodes. Did their strength fail them?" she asked.

"It would have. They tried to carry more than their strength permits."

"We are all heavily burdened."

"I see that," Hult said, glancing at the bundles clustered on the deck. "You leave Norion forever, then?"

She paused before replying, "We are leaving for a time."

"I heard the things that were said about the Remembrancers in Norion. They were lies."

"Too many believe them. It was not safe to stay."

The two elders, evodes of the little group, came to Hult's side. They gave the ritual greeting, and when he returned it, the older expressed their thanks for his help. "What may we offer you in return?" he asked.

"Have you a varasdode among you?"

"No," the woman replied. "We are mendodes and paturdodes, and the two evodes. No more. There are few varasdodes left in Norion."

"I need the memory of a varasdode. In return, I will assist you until the portage on the Upper Moharil."

"I must speak with the other women. If they know of a varasdode who might help us, we will accept your offer. Otherwise, we cannot repay," the leader said.

She left Hult with the evodes. He helped the two frail old men to arrange their bundles in the lee of the pile that occupied the center of the deck. They settled in, drawing their robes closer around them. Two young mendodes joined them, sitting at the feet of the old men.

The elder looked at Hult. "Now, for a time, we play at dur-ron-ag." He laid a hand affectionately on the head of each of the mendodes. "This game was begun by my tutor's tutor when he was younger than these two. Perhaps their pupils will see its end."

"Perhaps," Hult said. He had heard of the Remembrancers' complex game, but he knew—and cared—little about it. Dur-ron-ag was played entirely in the memory, and a single game lasted for generations, passed on from tutor to pupil. It served as discipline for the young, relaxation for the old, pleasure for all. But only a Remembrancer could hope to play such a game.

The elder closed his eyes and gave himself to quiet recollection. The others looked on attentively. At last he announced his pattern of play. "The Weaver ascends to the third level and proceeds unchecked to the space between the Two Towers. Here he waits. Beyond the Red Mountain, the Plainsmen gather and take the formation of Daldirian against the Altobod, but their leader is menaced by the Horned Riders. The Forcemaker gyrates. All who traverse the fifth level are in confusion. I give you these problems: First, locate the Wanderer and determine his identity. Second, close the descent from the sixth level without endangering the Novices. Third, stop the Weaver from passing beyond the Two Towers."

The mendodes looked at him with admiration. The other evode betrayed no reaction. He merely sat, silent, eyes closed, recalling to mind the moves and countermoves of three generations.

Many spoke of the Remembrancers' game with awe, but Hult was not impressed by it. To him, it seemed a waste of strength for such wise men as the evodes to play a game. Let mendodes and paturdodes use dur-ron-ag as a training device. The evodes were keepers of the myths, and should not squander their gift. So believed Hult, but he said nothing. It was not his affair.

A game of dur-ron-ag afforded little for the observer to watch. Hult left the four seated Remembrancers and went to the prow, where the air was coolest. In a little while the leader of the Remembrancers came to him.

"We cannot promise you the help of a varasdode. Perhaps one will be at the second portage to meet us, but this is not certain. Will you tell me what memories you wish?" she asked.

"I want to know what has befallen the Onhla since the time of the shaking sickness," Hult said.

"Yes, for that you need a varasdode. Tribes and races are his proper memories. But perhaps one of our mendodes can be of help. They carry memories of sickness and healing."

Hult considered the suggestion and rejected it. "The mendode can only tell me how many died. I would know more than that."

"Perhaps if you learn how many died, that will help you to know other things. Let the mendode offer his memories in gratitude for your help," the woman said.

Again, Hult rejected the offer. He had no need of the mendode's horde of memories. It would be pointless to listen while a youth recited tables of figures. Hult knew, in ways no outsider could comprehend, that all the Onhla but he had died in the plague and the madness that came after. What he wished to learn was the reaction to this news among the other Hraggellians, and its practical results.

A varasdode carried memories of tribes and clans and settlements, of the moving and shifting of groups across the face of the planet. If any had ventured into the Onhla hunting grounds, or sought to win the allegiance of the tormagons, a varasdode would know. If no varasdode could be found, it made little difference; Hult would learn the answers he sought soon enough. But he would have preferred, if possible, to know in advance. Those who lived in the cold country learned to avoid surprises whenever possible.

Since they could not repay his help with knowledge, the Remembrancers insisted on sharing their meal with Hult.

Fortunately for them, he was in a period of metabolic change, and ate only a handful of the fresh-caught gauntlings. Once his body was adjusted to the cold of the shadowlands, he would be able to consume half his weight in food at a sitting. The Remembrancers made no comment on the lack of appetite in someone of his size and bulk, but he sensed their curiosity.

After eating, he left the Remembrancers and settled into his former place by the prow. The raft was coming into the mists now, and the first faint touch of the wind from Starside could be felt in the air. The other passengers had all taken shelter, but Hult found the lower temperature invigorating and enjoyed it even more without shivering humans around him.

He sprawled against stacked cargo, looking ahead into the mist, his mind blank, totally at ease. Behind him, the murmur of the passengers rose and fell and then ceased entirely. After a brief silence, a single voice began a rhythmic chanting recitation of the Saga of Daldirian, so familiar to all the humans of Norion and the settlements. It was the elder evode whose voice Hult heard. The old man sang of Daldirian's voyage to the dark kingdom of Hrull in search of the beauteous Gliantha. This was one of the most familiar tales, a favorite in Norion. Hult had heard it often. He closed his eyes and listened, and before long he sank into a dreamless sleep.

They stopped not long after for their first rest. Oarsmen, crew, and passengers hurried ashore to the shelter of the warming huts. Hult stayed aboard the raft and slept on comfortably.

At the fifth stage, the portage for the Lesser Kariar, the miners left the company to journey up the Korkariar to the mountain orefields. Hult was glad to see them go. Like all Onhla, he despised those who work in the ground.

At the ninth stage, he went ashore and ate lightly. After that, he stayed at the prow, eyes fixed ahead, where the mouth of the Upper Moharil lay behind a thickening wall of mist.

Soon the cold whiteness enfolded the raft. The others drew their robes more closely around them, but Hult basked comfortably in the chill. The dark water grew turbulent, and the oarsmen pulled harder. The mouth of the river was near.

Twice again they came to shore, and the second time, all left the craft to continue the upriver journey. Beyond this point, sails were used no longer; indeed, the sails had hung limp during the passage through the mist, and been furled even before the craft reached the bank. The force of the galendergorn was not felt here. A cold wind came steadily down the valley of the Upper Moharil, strong in gusts, more often mild, but never ceasing. Added to the powerful current, it made travel on this portion of the river difficult, slow, and very costly. All power was supplied by professional oarsmen. Without them, there would be no transportation upriver, and the Upper Moharil was the safest route not only to the planting terraces but to all of shadowlands and Starside.

Hult had had his fill of human company. He elected to travel alone from this point on, following the caravan trail. At this time of the year there was no danger for a lone, unburdened traveler. It was at the time of second harvest and the shadowed days of lastlight, when hunters and miners returned to Norion with the takings of a lighttime's work, that the brigands and robbers struck. Now the trail was safe.

He set out at once, striding through the busy port settlement without a sideward glance, ignoring the calls of the various sellers of wares. He needed, and wanted, nothing from them. He wore all the clothing he required. His food could be found along the way; it was senseless to carry it. His weapons were on his wrists, and he used no tools. The calls of the women did not entice him; they were not Onhla.

The caravan trail ran parallel to the river for a time, then turned sharply to circle Lake Nesarla. Near the lake the way ran through thick forest, and here Hult first left the trail to hunt. He brought down a fleet young seexet, cooked it slowly over a low fire, and crowned the meal with his fill of long golden tridd berries. After eating, he found a shaded spot, and slept.

The next stretch of travel took him to higher ground. Here on the upland slopes he saw the first of the sunseekers in full bloom. They were an awesome sight for one who had no knowledge of these plants. But Hult saw only a familiar landmark.

Before him, like yawning caverns, spread scores of enormous black disks, that seemed to float just off the surface of the ground. The heart of each was aimed directly at Hraggellon's sun, a full forearm's length above the horizon. The interior, lined with countless velvety fingers of dull black, sucked in the warmth and light, generating food for storage in the plant's deep tuberous roots. Each lighttime, as the sun slowly climbed to its zenith, the sunseekers matched its ascent, until at midlight they pointed almost directly overhead, like a field of mighty trumpets in a silent fanfare. Then, as it sank, they bowed to the horizon, and closed tight when the sun disappeared at the final instant of lastlight. They grew even more thickly in the shadowlands, and their bitter tubers had often kept Onhla and tormagons alive through a time of poor hunting. To Hult, they were a welcome sign that he was drawing closer to his tribal grounds.

He traveled on, over ground carpeted with brilliant tiny flowerets, the unvarying light always at his back. The trail soon rejoined the river and then, after Hult had gone on for six more rests, it veered off once again. He followed it until he could see the twin mountains that rose beside the black lake, and then he left the caravan trail to follow the ancient path of the Onhla.

The sun was just over his right shoulder now. He went in this direction until a black lake lay like a dark mirror at his feet. This was the far boundary of the Onhla's grounds. It had no name; it was simply the dark water that few crossed. He hunted, and ate, and slept long and soundly on its shore, then plunged in and made the long swim to the opposite bank. No human could have survived in that icy water; to Hult, it was merely invigorating. He shook himself dry, then, with the sun once again at his back, he set out on the last long stretch of his journey.

Shadows lengthened as he went on, and the warmth of the sun became less noticeable. He traveled for longer marches now, and rested less often. When he crossed the last ragged range of low hills he stopped and sniffed deeply. The scent of tormagon was on the wind. He ranged them faintly, far ahead, and directed his steps toward them, loping along at a steady pace. He needed no rest now. He was home.

They scented him a long way off and bounded to greet him. Arll was still the pack leader, and he met Hult with all the ferocious affection of his kind. They growled and tussled and rolled on the soft ground. The others, hesitant at first, soon joined the welcome, and the noisy celebration went on until Arll called for a hunt and a feast of greeting.

As they sat in a ring, tearing chunks from the scorched seexets that lay in the ashes, Hult looked around for familiar faces of his cub days. Many were missing. Four darks had brought changes to the pack. Old Haggrap and Norlor, two of the strongest hunters, were gone, killed in a struggle with a herd of tulk. Arll himself carried a long scar from that costly hunt. There were few young hunters to replace the old stalwarts. One by one, they were being slain by humans, for their pelts. Cubs were few, and they looked scrawny. Bad times had come to the pack.

The problem was simple: food could not be taken as in times past. Without Hult to lead them, their old dread of Starside had returned. The ice-skimmers had gone too deep into Starside to be followed; the bucdyne, too, had withdrawn into the sanctuary of eternal ice and darkness. Tulk were seen more frequently now, but they had learned to defend themselves against tormagons. Soon the pack would be too small to hunt successfully in darktime, when the meat was best. For much of the dark just ended, they had lived on the tubers of the sunseeker. Some of the younger cubs had never tasted the meat of Starside beasts, only the commonplace seexet. Arll turned to Hult and expressed his sad belief that the tormagon would soon vanish, as the Onhla had done.

Hult spoke otherwise. If times were lean, and the old hunting grounds were not sustaining them, then they must look for new hunting grounds. They must return now to the cold of Starside and find new trails, new herds.

But the pack were reluctant. They had no wish to face the cold again. This was the time to head to the sun, not stay in the icy gloom. It was time to mate, to dive for the sweet-tasting water creatures, and enjoy the prickly fruits of the firebloom. Hult let them speak on, and when all had spoken, he said simply, "Do this, and in three darks the pack will be no more."

Arll said that this was true. The pack considered, and Gragunda, Arll's mate, asked what Hult recommended.

"I am on my way to Starside to hunt the gorwol. I need their pelts to take me to where other Onhla live. My way leads to a new hunting ground that only I know. Come with me. There will be food for all, in abundance," Hult said to them. "The pack will grow and prevail."

Arll agreed at once. Some of the old hunters, and the females who had known him as leader, respected Hult and were willing to follow his advice. Young hunters who had known him when they were cubs came to his side as he spoke, and believed his message.

Among creatures of instinct, Hult had grown up gifted with reason. The tormagons had the intelligence of children. They did not experiment or seek new ways. They did what had always been done, and when the old ways ceased to work, a pack died out. Arll had learned something from Hult, but Arll did not have sufficient intelligence to adopt Hult's methods and make them work.

Hult knew that there were reasons for good hunting times and bad. The creatures of Starside could not live always in Starside, for no food grew in those frozen wastes and the ice was too thick to break except at the outer edges. They had to leave Starside to feed, and if they were not coming to their accustomed feeding grounds it was because they had found new ones. Those who depended on the tulk, the ice-skimmer, and the bucdyne would have to follow them. So would he who sought the gorwol. If the way led through Starside it would be a hard trail, but there was no choice.

The pack took counsel and slept and took counsel again. At last it was decided that Hult and Arll would lead a small group of hunters into Starside while Gragunda took the rest into the light. The decision once reached, they wasted no time, but divided their food supply and left.

The sun sank behind the hunters. Eventually it disappeared below the horizon. Deeper and deeper into the ice and cold and darkness they went, the stars ever brighter and more numerous overhead. It was hard traveling. Their insulating layer of fat was all but used up, and their pelts had begun to thin, but the tormagon did not complain. They struggled on under the cheerless light of the far stars.

Hult knew the danger, and he moved them as quickly as he could. They were at the point of exhaustion when he crossed the mouth of the Great Rift, turned to the Brightside rim, and began to lead them back, toward the light. They wondered, but they did not question.

Supplies grew dangerously low, and game was scarce. They came upon a stray young bucdyne, but it was barely enough to fuel their bodies for the next march. A lone tulk was a tougher quarry, but it fed them well. With full bellies and a renewed meat supply, they moved on briskly. At last a slender golden wafer of sun lay on the horizon, and Hult pointed to the new hunting ground that rose out of the level field of white before them.

It was an island, safe from all hunters except those who could endure the long journey across the frozen seas of Starside. None but Onhla and tormagon could hope to reach it.

Over the ages, the beasts of Hraggellon had retreated ever farther into the dark and cold in their flight from hunters. The shadowlands were safe from humans, but pursued by the Onhla, the beasts fled into Starside, moving ever deeper into the wastes as the tribes still followed. Here on the island, some of them had found a haven. Hult had discovered it by pure chance when he strayed far from the known paths during his darks of solitary hunting. He had crossed the ice field and traveled far into the sun-lit lands beyond. There, on new and unknown ground, he found tulk and bucdyne in great number, and a small scattering of gorwol. He had hunted well, taken the pelts that were later stolen from him in his sickness, and turned back at midlight only to find that his return was cut off by a raging current of icy water that even an Onhla could not hope to oppose. He was trapped on the island until the first touch of darktime froze the waters for his safe crossing.

For most of the Hraggellian year, the narrow strait between the island and the main land mass of Starside lay in darkness, frozen solid. Human hunters could not cross the ice field and survive to reach the island; not without the help of an Onhla, and such help was not given humans. With the coming of light, the ice melted and the island was cut off from all approach, for the oceans of Hraggellon were beyond the power of man to navigate. Raging currents and unending gales made these waters the destruction of any craft known on the planet. The inland waterways were tame and useful; they furnished the chief means of transport on the planet. The rivers carried workers to their annual round at the coming of light, and the rivers bore them and their goods swiftly and safely to their enclosures before the fall of darkness. Nothing more was needed, and nothing more had ever been sought. The open seas were abandoned to ravaging beasts of the imagination, and life carried on in the band of alternating light and dark, along the riverbanks, and under the shelter of the city. The continents of Hraggellon were as isolated from one another as the five planets of their system.

Now the time for the breaking of ice was fast approaching. Hult led the tormagons forward over the smooth ice, up the low hills that rose beyond the shore line, and paused at the crest of the first peak. Below them, bathed in the early glow of the ascending sun, lay an open plain. Their keen eyes followed Hult's guiding gesture, and the pack beheld tiny specks far to sunward.

Hult took Arll's thick shoulder fur in his grip and said, "Come, old friend. Let us hunt."

Arll growled low, eager and happy at the abundance awaiting them. Smoothly, swiftly, the hunters descended the hillside and crossed the plain. Hunger was behind them now. The hunt was on.

Shedding of fur is the first sign of the coming of haldrim. As the childhood coat works off, sexual characteristics develop and the Onhla acquires a human appearance. Heaviness of body, particularly in the upper back, results from a developing layer of subcutaneous fat. This heaviness plus a flatter face with heavy bone ridges over and beside the eyes and thick tufts of hair below the eyes are the chief distinguishing marks of the race, although many Onhla in haldrim appear completely human. They lose a certain amount of their natural resistance to cold during early haldrim, but are still capable of enduring temperatures colder than any humanoid race on record.

We are aware of no detectable difference between a pure-blood Onhla and the child of a mixed Onhla-outsider marriage, but Onhla are said to discriminate absolutely. They treat the children of such marriages as outcasts, and bar them from tribal grounds and ceremonies. As far as we can determine, there are no circumstances under which marriage between an Onhla and an outsider is permissible to the Onhla.

Regarding a possible third Onhla life-phase, we have been unable to find definite proof. . . .

Soman Wirsing, Secondary

Fourth Hraggellon Contact Mission

V.

SPACE

With the first closing of the floodgates, the Moharil diminished to a trickle. Soon the heat of midlight turned
Norion into an oven. The ramps and galleries were almost
empty, and the city lay silent under the full hot blast of the
galendergorn. In all the downriver settlements, outside activity ceased and life retreated behind thick walls until the
time for second planting. Clell Basedow spent most of the
midlight period sprawled on his sleeping platform, bemoan-
ing the cruel irony that sends a man to die of heat exhaustion on a frostworld.

But Seb Dunan kept busy in spite of the heat. He roamed
the deserted city, wandered along the riverbank and the
quays, among the deepest banks of cisterns, even visited the
farming settlements, always alert for trade. At every stop he
looked, and asked, and listened. More than once he was on
the brink of exhaustion, but he drove himself on. This mission had to succeed, and there was no success without hard
work. His efforts served a second purpose as well: they
helped to keep his thoughts from the Onhla and the disturbing events in Norion.

The heat of midlight passed. The floodgates opened once
again, the river rose, and the second crop was planted. Second harvest came, and then the poignant longshadowed
dusk of lastlight. The fall of dark was near. It was time for
the wanderers to return to Norion, time for the traders to
leave Hraggellon. Seb Dunan could no longer avoid facing
his doubts.

Should have gotten his name, at least, he told himself a
dozen times between waking and sleeping. And no sooner
had he admonished himself than he realized the absurdity of
it. What help would the Onhla's name be? If the hunter

chose not to return, would knowing his name enable me to drag him here? Or make it possible for anyone to cross the shadowlands and drag him out of Starside? I'm being a fool, he admitted. He'll be back. He's given his word. And besides, he wants that trip to Insgar more than anything else, and I'm the only one who can provide it.

If he thought that even one Onhla woman remained alive on this planet, Dunan would have been desolated. He knew enough about the tribesmen to know that his hunter, with those inexplicable Onhla senses, would have found her somehow, and lost all desire to visit Insgar. But Dunan had sought out varasdodes who knew all there was to know about the tribes and races of Hraggellon, and they had assured him that the Onhla were extinct. He tried not to let the fact that they were wrong about one undermine his faith in their over-all accuracy. He had to believe them.

The varasdodes had not been easy to find. They were never numerous in Norion, but since the coming of Orm, all levels of Remembrancers were becoming scarce in the city. Dunan found their departure easy to understand, having on three separate occasions seen the treatment they received from Orm's public guardians. He still did not understand the reason for the new regime's implacable hatred of the Remembrancers. They were a harmless, necessary people, and Norion would soon feel their loss.

Orm, he was coming to believe, was a fool. He had the fool's universal fear and hatred of superiority, the fool's conviction of his own absolute righteousness, the fool's belief in force to accomplish all ends. Clell seemed to consider him a giant among men; that in itself was enough to raise serious doubts about Orm's worth. But Orm's rule would end, as did all others. Seb Dunan foresaw the pattern: Orm would overstep himself in a short time, be deposed or murdered, and the Sternverein would be ready to deal equally with his successor before the blood had dried. It was a bad business.

Dunan looked forward eagerly to liftoff from this sorry world.

The sun was a mere lozenge of light on the horizon when Dunan and his assistant placed their personal effects aboard the white driveship *Grixlingen* and settled down to await the Onhla's arrival. Dunan was silent, thoughtful, concerned with the stowage of the light-globes, the survival of the hundreds of clingers and plants and seedlings he had acquired, and the whereabouts of the Onhla. Clell Basedow was no help at all. He seemed to have uncovered a rich vein of calamitous possibilities, and Dunan let him rant on unchecked. The Onhla had forgotten. The Onhla had betrayed them and sold his pelts to others. No more gorwol were to be found. The Onhla was not a true tribesman, but a half-blood set to deceive them by rival traders. The Onhla had died in Starside. He had been waylaid, and his pelts stolen. He had lost his way and would not return in time. And so on, endlessly, until Seb Dunan wearily told his assistant to be quiet.

"But what if he doesn't come? We don't know his name. How can we look for him in darktime? Where would we look?" Clell went on.

"He'll be here. We can give him a little time," Dunan said patiently.

"It's all but darkfall now. The floodgates are closing. They may already be closed. He told us he'd—"

"I know what he said. I also know he wants very much to get to Insgar, and we're the only ones who can bring him there. Be patient, Clell, and stop worrying. We'll get the furs."

That sent Basedow off on a new tack. "But look what we're paying for them. An intersystem trip is worth a lot. There'll be trouble about this agreement of yours, I'm afraid."

"What trouble? One gorwol pelt would pay that Onhla's

way across the galaxy. We're getting six. I don't expect trouble, I expect a great deal of gratitude."

Clell frowned and made ready to explore a new avenue of
possible woe, but he had no opportunity. A crewman came
to the cabin to notify them that a big native was at the landing ring with a bundle on his shoulder, and was asking for
the old trader. For the first time, Dunan realized that while
he had fretted all through lighttime for having forgotten to
ask the Onhla's name, the tribesman had not been at all interested in determining his. In a burst of relief and high
spirits, he laughed aloud and hurried to the boarding ramp.
Clell followed closely, still silent. This has been too much
for him, Dunan thought happily. Might shut him up for a
good long time. That made the doubts worth while.

The Onhla was waiting at the foot of the ramp. He received Dunan's hearty greeting impassively, saying only, "I
have the gorwol furs. I wish to leave now."

"You will, my friend. We'll lift off at once, if that's
agreeable."

"It is," said the Onhla, and stepped to the ramp. Without
a backward glance, he ascended to the main port.

Clell was at Dunan's elbow, fretting and whispering.
"You shouldn't let him go aboard until you've checked the
furs. How do you know what furs are in that bundle, or how
many? You let him walk on board as if he owned the *Grixlingen*."

Dunan kept his patience with an effort. "If he's cheated
us, we can throw him off the ship. I believe he lived up to
his agreement. He's not civilized enough to be a swindler."

"Well, he's on the ship now. And if he's delivered six gorwol pelts, we have to bring him all the way to Insgar and
back. I don't see why we have to bother—"

"We have to do it because we agreed to do it," Dunan
broke in. "A trader keeps his word, even when it hurts him,
because if he doesn't, it will hurt him a lot more. There's no

trade for liars, Clell, and if you learn only that and nothing else on this trip, you've still learned a lot."

"Well, I still think—"

"Shut up and get aboard. We have a long trip ahead of us," Dunan said curtly. As his assistant made ready a remonstrance, he added, "One more stupid suggestion about cheating the only supplier of gorwol pelts on this planet, and I'll leave you here until we get back."

Basedow was up the ramp like a rocket.

They examined the furs in Dunan's cabin. The Onhla had delivered at his word, and the sight of the shimmering pale smoke-colored furs was so far beyond Dunan's expectations that he could only stare in wonderment. Even his assistant was awed into a momentary silence.

Unrolled, the gorwol furs seemed to come alive, expanding to their fullness at the release of pressure. Dunan reached out reverently to sink his fingers in the silvery glow, and plunged his hand in past the wrist before he touched the dense underfleece. The long upper hairs fell like a warm breeze against his skin. He slid his hands under the pelt and lifted it, and the thick fur, nearly six square meters in area, floated upward at his touch, almost weightless despite its bulk. The surface flashed a dazzling blaze of light as the fur moved, and seemed to emit a cool glow from deep within itself. It was a magnificent object. Incredible that it comes from a stupid, clumsy beast like a gorwol, Dunan thought. Beauty like that from such a creature, on a world like this. The galaxy sometimes made no sense at all.

"They're the most beautiful things I've ever seen," Basedow said in a hushed voice. "No wonder the Sternverein wants them."

"Everybody in the galaxy wants them. Do you still begrudge the hunter his trip to Insgar?"

For one instant, Clell Basedow was generous. "No. They're worth it a hundred times over. But can we be sure he'll get us more? Can we make him deal exclusively with us?"

"I think so," Dunan said.

"If we can't, and if headquarters see these furs and finds that we've allowed—"

"Leave it to me," Dunan broke in. "For the time being, just try to appreciate the furs we've got. We have too long a trip ahead of us to spend it worrying about all the things that can go wrong."

Dunan's advice proved sound. The voyage to Insgar was uneventful. Once the jump to drivespeed was accomplished, the *Grixlingen* moved in a dimensionless gray tunnel, silent, lightless, featureless. The passengers and crew had no sensation of speed, or even of motion. Intersystemic travel was not an adventure; it was primarily a matter of patiently enduring the passage of time.

The Onhla had been placed in a small storage bin against the outer hull, the coolest spot on the ship. He kept to his quarters and spoke to no one unnecessarily. It was customary for a driveship crew to inflict a certain amount of harassment on a newcomer to deep-space travel, but somehow no one seemed interested in initiating the old custom in the case of the silent, unsmiling Onhla. He was left to himself.

Hult was an intimidating figure. He had added a good deal of bulk to his frame since his departure for the hunting grounds, and the long period of strenuous activity had firmed it into solid muscle. His appearance now was nothing short of majestic. The hair of his cheekbones, just below the eyes, had grown out in full and he wore it in the Onhla fashion. It swept down on either side of his jaw in a golden arc to blend with the brown and gold ruff that encircled his neck and shoulders. He was newly outfitted in splendid furs of brown and gold, and an even richer outfit was safely packed away for his use on Insgar. Out of the cold of Starside, the pale blue-white of his skin was deepening to the ruddy coloration of Dunan and his assistant. In his manner, above all else, Hult was aloof and apart from everyone else on the *Grixlingen*. He seemed to see sights and hear sounds that they could not, to move easily through dimensions they could only half perceive and could not understand at all. In the ages of life in the cold and darkness of Hraggellon's wastelands, his people had developed senses and sensitivities unknown to others on the planet. But Hult's shipmates did not take into account the shaping force of time and climate and necessity. They saw an alien and shunned him.

All but Seb Dunan. He was genuinely interested in Hult, not only as a source of wealth but as a creature unique in his experience. The other aliens he had met—and he knew scores of them—had never seemed quite as alien as this Onhla tribesman. It was not a matter of appearance, for Hult, in his present stage, looked much like an exceptionally big human of the Old Earth lineage. Nor was it language, for he spoke the common tongue without any of the distracting hums, whistles, and clicks Dunan had been forced to decipher on other worlds. It was something far deeper than these superficial differences, and it puzzled and fascinated the trader.

Hult was not as easily fascinated. Watch after watch he remained apart, unseen, venturing inward from time to time for an enormous meal and returning at once to his quarters. Dunan's patience grew strained, but he did not press the Onhla, and at last he was rewarded. After a watch-long conference with the *Grixlingen's* defender, who had once visited Insgar, he returned to his cabin and found the Onhla waiting.

Hult was seated with his back against the cool bulwark. His greeting was straightforward. "Tell me of Insgar," he said.

Dunan tried to conceal his surprise at the question, coming, as it did, when he had just finished an informal course of instruction on the planet. Could the Onhla read minds?

The creature revealed nothing, merely waited for a reply, and Dunan finally said, "I'll tell you all I can. But I want you to tell me some things in return. What do you want to know about Insgar?"

"When my people were brought there, and why. Where they dwell now, and how I can find them. Tell me these things first."

"As I said, I'll tell you what I can. I don't know the answers to all your questions, though." Dunan thought for a moment, recalling the data he had found in the ship's information center, then began, "Onhla were brought to Insgar around the year 2706 of the Galactic Standard Calendar. Insgar was said to have valuable fur-bearing animals in the polar regions. It doesn't have the extremes of heat and cold that you find on Hraggellon, but the poles are still too cold for anyone but an Onhla, so the Onhla were brought there to hunt."

"What tribes?"

"The records don't show," Dunan said.

"Was it long ago?"

"Nearly two centuries, by the Galactic Standard Calendar. A fairly long time. Approximately . . . oh, about two hundred and eighty to three hundred Hraggellian darks," Dunan said, calculating rapidly. When the Onhla spoke, Dunan realized that the dates and figures meant nothing to him.

"How many lifetimes?"

Dunan held up three fingers. "This many, in Norion. I don't know how long Onhla live."

Hult was silent for a time, then he asked, "What is Insgar?"

"It's a planet like Hraggellon, but with a different kind of year. It rotates . . . it has a much shorter day than its year, not both of them the same, as on Hraggellon. Darks and lights follow one another much more rapidly on Insgar. I can show you what I mean easier than explain it. Do you know about planets and planetary systems?"

"We know that the Maker of Weathers created many cold places. Some are on Hraggellon, some are far away. All are one."

"Some are *very* far away. Do you have any idea how far it is from Hraggellon to Insgar?" Dunan asked.

"Too far for us. But the otherworlders have brought us a way to travel, and now we can go to the other places, if we so choose."

Dunan rubbed his bald pate thoughtfully and said nothing. Such casual acceptance of interstellar flight was something he had not experienced before. The townsmen of Norion had cringed before the first starfarers on their planet, but this primitive hunter coolly received starflight as a convenient gift. It appeared that Onhla truly were incapable of fear. Dunan had heard this said, but until now he had not believed it. Again, he felt the touch of alienness. He despaired of ever understanding a mind so different from his own; nevertheless, he persisted.

"Starflight is not ordinary travel. It's not like going up the Moharil or crossing shadowlands. The power and the speed involved are beyond imagining. Even time is affected, *that's* how different it is." He paused, anticipating some reaction, but the Onhla showed none. He went on, "When we return to Hraggellon, more time will have passed for the Hreggellians than for us aboard the *Grixlingen*. Much more time. I don't know how it works. I'm no scientist. Even the scientists don't fully understand it, but we all know it happens. Do you have any idea what I'm talking about?" Dunan concluded helplessly.

"Yes. This happens to Onhla . . . sometimes."

Dunan could think of nothing more than, "Does the thought of time lapse bother you?"

"No. More time for the gorwol to increase."

Dunan grunted in reply, then said, "Well, I'm glad you're taking to drivespeed so nicely."

Hult ignored the pleasantry. "Tell me about the Onhla of Insgar. Where do they dwell and how shall I find them?"

"All I know is what the ship's defender told me. He said that the hunting seems to have died out. Most of the Onhla are mining now."

"Onhla, mining?" There was surprise in Hult's voice.

"Yes. Placer mining, in the spring floods. They're the only ones who can endure the temperature."

"Onhla do not work with the dead things of the inner land. They must work with living things. The ship's defender lied to you."

"Maybe the Onhla have changed their ways since coming to Insgar," Dunan suggested.

"If they change, they are Onhla no longer."

"Don't judge them until you see them. I'm only telling you what someone else told me."

"Does he say that all the Onhla have stooped to working with dead things?"

"He said most, not all. He was not sent there to learn about the Onhla, so he did not seek to find out more. The best thing for you to do is go directly to the orefields and ask," Dunan advised.

Hult was silent, abstracted for a time, then he asked, "How long to Insgar?"

"It's three hundred and nineteen watches from Hraggellon. We're more than halfway there," Dunan said. Remembering the Onhla's ignorance of their ways of calculation, he explained, "We're nearer now to Insgar than to Hraggellon."

Hult stood up, as if to leave. Dunan raised a hand. "Wait. You said you'd answer my questions."

"Some things we do not tell outsiders," the tribesman warned.

"I don't want any of your tribal secrets. First tell me your name."

"I did not ask yours."

"No, you didn't. All right, then, no names. How many gorwol are left? Can you tell me that?"

Hult extended the fingers of both hands. "More than this."

"This many?" Dunan asked, extending his own fingers twice in succession.

"Perhaps. I did not see so many."

"Are they in danger of dying out?"

"No. The gorwol are safe."

"Good. Listen, hunter, I understand why you're going to Insgar, and I wish you success. I'll give you what help I can. If you do find Onhla there, and you all go back to Hraggellon and rebuild the tribes, will you agree to trade gorwol furs only with me and the people I send to you?"

"I will agree. I cannot bind the others."

"Will you try to make them agree? All I ask is that you try."

"I will try," Hult said.

When the Onhla had left, Dunan lay in his narrow bunk. He opened the scent-case and breathed deeply, to bring up his strength. He needed the stimulant much more lately. Feeling tired, often exhausted, ready to drop. Trying to do too much. But with an assistant like Clell, a mission like this, there was just too much to do. At least the worst was over.

The presence and manner of the big tribesman had been unnerving. Dunan was soaked in perspiration and his insides felt knotted. An absurd reaction, he thought. Thanks to me, this creature has the chance to rebuild his race. If he succeeds, I may become one of their demigods. He laughed his silent laugh at the thought of it. A fat old trader, a Sternverein drudge, and I'll be immortal. But he's frightening, all the same, Dunan admitted to himself. Friendly or not—and who can tell one from the other with an Onhla?—he scares me. So much in there, deep in his mind, that will never come out for an otherworlder, or anyone but an Onhla. I wonder how they act toward one another?

He thought about that for a few moments, and then the Onhla's plight burst upon him with a clarity that tore at his heart. There were no others. This silent, secretive giant was the last of his kind. After Insgar, there was no more for him, no future but solitude.

It was not the thought of the loneliness that Dunan found so fearful. He had been alone all his life, a man without family or close friends. He had not even a homeworld. Such ties were not possible for starfarers. To leave a wife, children, friends, a world, behind while one ventured into space was to abandon them to time while one escaped its passage. Return was too painful.

But despite all that, Dunan would always have others of his kind to speak with. They existed, if he chose to seek them out; he was not truly alone. The awful isolation of the tribesman would be too much to bear. The Onhla had to be there on Insgar, he thought, and they have to be true Onhla still. Anything else would be worse than the worst death imaginable.

JANUSAITIS SYSTEM: PLANET TWO
Gravity: 1.09 OES
Diameter: 12,160 k.
Rotation: 19.25 hours GSC
Revolution: 349.52 days GSC
Atmosphere: N77.49; 021.68; breathable and
                          safe for Types 4 through 13
Planetary analogues: Shantelaine; Sutt-23b-Griph

The name of the planet is INSGAR. First mention, 2361; first charting, 2519; Pioneer Mission, 2609; first contact, *SD Keersha* in 2679. An industrial world; six landing rings, full base facilities; independent.

Ref: Sternverein chart 716603B-85A-G4

VI.

INSGAR

The old trader tried to advise him of the differences between Insgar and Hraggellon, but Hult could spare no time to listen. He knew his capacities. If adjustments were necessary, his body would adjust; if it could not, then he would suffer. Other Onhla had survived here; so would he. What must be done would be done, and it was foolish to talk about things that talking could not change. They agreed on a rendezvous, and Hult left the *Grixlingen* to begin his search.

He noticed several major differences almost at once. Light and dark came in rapid succession on this world, and the temperature remained relatively stable. That was an advantage, since it required no adjustment from his shipboard state. But the noise was very bad, and the air, at times, was worse.

Insgar was a far different place from Hraggellon or the sparsely populated wilderness world the earlier Onhla had come to. Structures the size of Hraggellian settlements rose everywhere. Hult saw one nearly the size of Norion, giving off spurts of fire and columns of dark smoke. The breeze that blew past it, bearing his craft upriver to the orefields, carried a burden of heavy fumes. It was a bad smell, the stench of the dead things of the underground that Onhla were forbidden to touch or traffic with.

The smoke seemed to be an omen, for the early news that came to Hult was discouraging. At one site after another he was told that Onhla no longer worked the streams. They had been replaced by machines that did the work faster and better, and never needed rest. Where the Onhla had gone, no one knew or cared. They were somewhere upriver; no one could tell him more than that.

Hult traveled on, and wherever he went, the roar and stink of machinery assaulted his senses. A painful ambivalence grew in his mind: much as he longed for the sight of fellow Onhla, he dreaded to find them defiled by contact with forbidden things. But this, at last, was what he found.

He stopped at a remote encampment and made his customary inquiry. No one recognized the name "Onhla," but they told him of others who resembled him and spoke a speech like his. Hult followed the directions given him, and after some days of travel arrived at a small camp high in the mountains. He heard the sounds of machinery long before he smelled the first fumes or saw the rising tongues of flame against the darkening sky.

There were many Onhla in this camp, and they welcomed him as a kinsman. But they were not kin to him, for in Hult's eyes they were Onhla no longer. They had embraced a forbidden way of life, breaking the surface of a world and drawing forth dead substances to barter with outsiders.

They heard Hult's words, and he theirs, but they did not communicate with one another. Those of the camp looked at Hult's garments curiously, remembering the garments of their elders, the dress of the homeworld. Their own garments were dull and dirty, fit for the smoke and dust of Insgar. They wore no fur, no tribal colors. Even the tribal coloration of their hair had faded and dulled to a uniform nondescript brownish-black. Their wrists were bare; at their sides hung blades made of dead stuff from beneath the ground. They slept within walls. They dressed like humans, and were fast coming to look like humans. Already they had come to think in human ways, as Hult soon learned.

The Onhla gathered after the fall of dark. Hult, as the newcomer, spoke first, and told them of his journey and his purpose. No sooner had he spoken than a voice demanded, "Where are the others?"

"There are no others. I am the last," he replied, and went on to tell of the shaking sickness and the death of the tribes.

For a long time there was silence, then a different voice said, "You did wisely to leave that dead world to the dreamers. Here, you can live well. No more hunting for the Onhla of this world. We take our riches from the ground."

"That is forbidden," Hult said.

The response was quick and defiant. "It was forbidden on Hraggellon. Enough lay above the ground to sustain us all. This is Insgar, and other laws prevail. Our elders tried to live here as they had on the homeworld, and they suffered much. We do not suffer."

"I follow the ways of Hraggellon. I have come to my haldrim, and I must have a partner if my tribe is to endure. Since no more Onhla live on Hraggellon, I came here to seek a partner and return with her to the homeworld. Tell me now: are there Onhla who have kept the ways of Hraggellon?"

Another long silence followed, and then one of the Onhla arose to respond. His voice was harsh as he said, "We are of Insgar. The ways of Hraggellon do not bind us. We have no tribes and hold no Great Gathering. Long ago, I heard of some who did otherwise. They went to the cold places to await the time of return. Seek them."

"Do they live still?" Hult asked.

"Seek them," the other replied, and then said no more.

Despite his differences with the others, Hult was made welcome in their camp. The old tradition of shelter to wayfarers had not been abandoned with the other homeworld ways. He was well fed and given a choice cold place to sleep for as long as he wished to stay.

Hult remained in the camp only one full day and left at dawn for the polar lands. The camp and its residents troubled him. He felt himself among strangers, and wanted more than ever to find true Onhla, if they survived.

The directions were simple, and the way was easy until he reached a point where the days were noticeably shorter and the snows lay deep. Here he found no more trails, but the surroundings were more comfortable for him. They were like the shadowlands of Hraggellon; good country for Onhla. He began to hope again.

With the drop in temperature, his appetite increased. He found the wild game sufficient, and easily caught all he needed. Game became scarcer as he approached the polar region, but he had no difficulty in filling himself on the fat burrowing creatures. Their flesh was sweet and filling. Still, he saw no sign of Onhla life.

He pressed on, ever deeper into the cold and lengthening darkness, and found himself drawn to a certain low range of mountains. No one at the camp, no one on Insgar, had mentioned the mountains, but Hult felt a growing conviction that they held the surest way to his goal.

He crossed an open tundra, into a buffeting wind that roared down a long valley, and began his ascent. At nightfall on the second day of climbing he stopped, perplexed, and felt a vague disturbance. He sensed that he was close to his goal, but was somehow missing his direction. When light came again, he descended to the foot of the mountain and worked his way to the base of the highest peak. Here he began to ascend once again, this time with complete assurance that his objective was at hand. He could not say how he knew. He knew, and that was all.

There, at the entrance to a cave, he found the Onhla. Crouched at the cave mouth was an ancient far into his nithbrog, the rare third stage of Onhla life. This was the first ancient Hult had ever seen.

The creature was twice Hult's size and richly robed in the colors of a tribe unknown on Hraggellon. The skin of its face and hands was deep blue; its hair and the billowing ruff around its neck were dazzling white. Around the shoulders hung a cloak of gorwol skin; beneath it was a tightly woven band of knotted leather strips, a tribal history of great age. The ancient spoke slowly, with some difficulty. Its voice boomed out like the slow beating of a great drum.

"We have waited long. Proclaim your tribe," the ancient said in formal greeting.

"I am Hult of the Bachan, who share colors with the Zabrosse and the Kleto."

"Come closer," said the ancient. It took long to study Hult, peering closely at his features and attire and running sensitive finger tips over the undervest of knotted leather. Hult felt the power touching his mind, but did not resist. No one could resist the mental power of one in nithbrog.

Its investigation done, the ancient motioned Hult back and said, "Your tribe and history belong to the homeworld."

"I am from Hraggellon. There I reached my haldrim, and I came here to seek my partner."

"The knots tell of great suffering on the homeworld, sickness and killing without reason. Is this why you came to Insgar?" the ancient asked. "Are you in flight?"

"I came because I am the last Onhla of Hraggellon."

"Then it is fulfilled!" the ancient burst out in a voice that rolled among the peaks. "All have been swept from the homeworld, and now the Bachan of Hraggellon and the Jengg of Insgar will create a new tribe and a new race!"

"I know of no such prophecy," Hult said. He spoke not to challenge the ancient but merely to admit his own ignorance. An Onhla who attained nithbrog enjoyed knowledge from sources unknown to others. Communication was difficult. An ancient might be misunderstood; it might speak things beyond all comprehension; but its words were never doubted.

"No prophecy. A foreknowing. The change had already begun among us of Insgar when I came to nithbrog, and the Onhla ways were in danger. Before my birth, a leader of the Jengg brought those who would listen to these cold places, where they kept the true Onhla ways alive. The others stayed below and learned the life of outsiders," the ancient explained.

"I saw them and spoke with them. They dig in the ground and have no colors."

"It was to come," the ancient said, its great voice subdued now, the note of triumph gone. "Life here has been harder than the life on the homeworld. Often we hungered, and some returned to the camps below to trade their heritage for the new comforts. But others endured. I kept them strong because I knew you would come. Even this day, I knew you would come. And now you are here." The ancient arose, towering over Hult. "Come, and be seen by Treborra," it said, turning to lead Hult into the cave.

Hult's eyes dilated in the darkness, and he saw the form that lay on the low platform on a bed of furs. It was a female, young, barely into the fullness of her haldrim. She rose to greet him, and the ancient withdrew.

The Onhla did not entertain such concepts as love, and their language contained no words for the softer emotions. Their way of life had made other qualities more desirable. Hult saw these qualities in the woman before him. The ripeness of her body and the brilliance of her tribal coloration showed vitality, and the clarity and wisdom in her eyes proclaimed one who would nurture a tribe to surpass all who had lived before them. Hult knew he had found a partner at last, and a partner worth all the seeking.

Treborra, in her turn, studied Hult and approved. The colors of his mane glowed with life. He had the strong figure of a hunter, and only a skilled and cautious hunter could have taken the furs he wore. He was young, but he had shown great wisdom and determination. To find Treborra, he had crossed the stars. The greatest part of his haldrim time still lay ahead, as did hers. Together they could build a great tribe.

Though the outcome was known to both, ritual remained to be observed. This was no Great Gathering, with scores of young competing for the honor of creating new life. Treborra was the last female of her tribe, guarded by the last ancient, and sought by the last Onhla of the homeworld. Even so, Hult had to prove himself worthy, and she had to express her choice freely.

She laid a hand on the thick ruff around his neck, digging her fingers deep into the barred brown and gold of his mane. The other hand she pressed against his chest. For a moment her hands rested on him, then she turned away and drew herself up. "Provide," she commanded.

Hult raced from the cave, careering down the mountain-side in a small avalanche of fresh-fallen snow. No others contested him on this world, as they would at a Great Gathering, but honor still demanded the utmost in speed and skill.

From the foot of the mountain he set off across the snows like a polar wind. His Onhla senses had gathered much knowledge of the creatures of this world, and he knew where he would find the best meat and the thickest furs. But he wanted more than that.

He soon reached the ridge that overhung the forest of low, thick-trunked trees, and there he paused to send forth his power. Like slim groping fingers, uncertain at first but rapidly growing strong and sure, his hunting senses reached out to the dwellers in this cold world. He soon found the life he sought. Fitfully and wordlessly, the reactions filtered back.

Hult sank low and moved into the forest. His first quarry were the fat, short-legged burrowers whose flesh was so succulent. He came upon a huddled, trembling clutch of the creatures, and placing a stillness upon them he dispatched them quickly and without pain. Twice more he took meat and furs, then he stopped. He felt a new response.

He rested for a time, clearing his mind completely, then he focused once again. He had taken food and pelts; now he sought hunting companions.

The koomiok, the white stalkers of Insgar, were quick to sense the challenge that came upon them out of nowhere. They knew not how, but suddenly they felt a strong new presence in their familiar hunting grounds. It offered an alliance unlike any they had ever known, and this was beyond their comprehension. The presence had to be confronted at once, or accepted forever. They hesitated, confused, and some fled. But others turned to fight for their territory.

They slipped through the forest noiselessly, moving under the low boughs and across the open spaces, homing in on the newcomer. Hult heard no sound, but he ranged the creatures at his back, closing in fast, one on either hand. The koomiok did not possess a ranging sense, and since they came silently from upwind, behind the interloper's back, they expected to strike without warning.

But Hult had them located, and felt them drawing near. Another brushed his ranging sense, but this one was far off, just within the limits of perception; no threat as yet. The two who neared had come to resist; he felt that at once. He wished for a close look, one chance to study their movements and their natural armament and methods of attack, but that was impossible without giving away his readiness. He had glimpsed several koomiok from afar on his way to the mountains, but had never seen them hunt. He soon would.

He sat motionless by his kill, in the center of the little clearing, until the first of the stalkers burst from the forest to launch itself at his back. In one smooth motion he slapped the blade free from his wrist, flicked it to firmness, and rose, turning to face the creature's attack. Again, he offered the chance for alliance. The koomiok received it and rejected it in a burst of rage. It wanted no relationship but hunter and hunted.

The koomiok's claws were dilated, big forepaws raised to beat the quarry down while the stalker's broad jaws closed on his neck. Hult was too fast. He sidestepped the rush and brought the flat of his blade hard down on the stalker's broad skull. The thing staggered uncertainly on hind legs. Hult ducked beneath a claw and ripped the koomiok from crotch to throat with one slash, then yanked it forward to drain its life into the snow while he saw to the next attacker.

The second stalker was more cautious. It rushed into the clearing, then dropped low, its neck arched backward, head up to present Hult with a double row of long teeth. Hult snarled his defiance at the thing and it spat hatred back at him. It moved quickly and smoothly from side to side, darting forward to feint an attack and then backward to safety, studying Hult's moves and weapons even as he studied its own. Hult crouched and freed the blade from his other wrist. Firming it, he dropped both arms and gripped the blades by the midpoint, swinging them parallel to the snow, forward and back, in a rhythmic rocking motion. The stalker brought its head lower, opened its jaws to strike at one taunting hand, and Hult let the blade fly with all his strength, directly down the creature's throat. The koomiok reared upward, clawing at him and at the agony that burned within it, and Hult slashed it open with the same swift vertical stroke and flung it to the snow to die.

The pelts were undamaged. He could present Treborra with two fine furs and a long supply of food, but more was necessary. Hult had to know that he had not won by default. He wanted to perform some feat that would set him apart from all the suitors in all the Great Gatherings of the Onhla's knotted history.

The other stalkers had fallen back, and he sensed their presence no longer. At once he set to skinning the two he had slain, working quickly and with great skill to bring the skins loose unmarred and clean of all flesh. When they were ready he hung them high and carried the carcasses far off. Returning, he took half the meat of the burrowers and buried it in the snow before him, then all was ready.

He sent his power forth, pressing for contact. Perhaps he could not penetrate the mental patterns of creatures of another world, but he meant to try. The stalkers were not so different from things he had hunted on Hraggellon. They had reacted to his probe. He thought communication possible, and worth the attempt, if he could only bring them close enough.

He ranged them coming from all directions. They came singly and in pairs, moving smoothly and cautiously to where the new unfearing creature drew them. This time the stalkers did not attack. They squatted before Hult in the snow, looked at the white pelts hanging overhead and the bloody patches on the ground, and waited. He felt their curiosity and uneasiness.

When he ranged no more in the forest, Hult made contact with the stalkers as he had once spoken to a tormagon pack. Their language was simple, and he learned much from their mental responses and motions. He communicated more directly as he went on. Some snarled and rose to bare their teeth in defiance. He raised his blades, pointed to the skins that hung drying, and restated his message. They sank back. Two of the smallest stalkers left the rest and crept toward him, heads lowered in obeisance. Two more followed, then others. Finally, those who had begun by defying him came to his feet. He stood in triumph for a moment, the koomiok abject before him, then he reached down, uncovered the cache of meat he had prepared, and bade them eat. When they were filled, he took the remaining meat and the pelts on his own shoulders. With a command to follow, he turned and started for the cave where Treborra waited.

The ancient sat by the entrance as before, and once again it led Hult to Treborra. He had done her bidding and returned with proof of his abilities. She looked with approval on his trophies.

"The koomiok are dangerous. Only the best hunters take their pelts. Never has a lone hunter taken two," she said.

She extended her hands to Hult. Before she could speak the words of acceptance, he said, "I bring more. Come and see."

She followed him to the cave mouth and looked below. At the foot of the mountain, the koomiok sat in a semicircle. At Hult's silent command, they looked up and gave a shrill hollow cry.

"I bring my hunting pack," Hult said.

"No Onhla has ever mastered the koomiok," Treborra said, looking at him with new admiration. "You are my choice, Hult. We will make a new tribe together."

"Not on Insgar. This is a poor world. Come back to Hraggellon. All the Onhla are gone. The tormagon are without masters. The gorwol and the tulk grow lazy and unwary. The homeworld will be ours, to pass on to our tribe."

She laid her hands on his shoulders and pressed her cheek against his mane. "You are my partner forever. We will go to Hraggellon," she said.

For a time, they lived in the high cave. The days were passed in hunting with the koomiok. At the fading of the light Treborra and Hult returned to the cave, and after they ate, they listened to the ancient, groping for the wisdom that underlay the cryptic utterances. At night, Hult and Treborra lay in close union on the platform piled with furs, while the ancient kept vigil at the entry.

It was an interlude of great contentment for Hult. He had risked much, and succeeded. Two darks of degradation within the walls of Norion and a long journey across the emptiness had brought him to a fine partner. Much had been fulfilled on Insgar, and as the time for their departure drew near, there was a promise of more to come. Treborra had already sensed the life of a new Onhla moving within her.

One evening the ancient told them that all had been completed and they would be alone from this night on. Others awaited on the mountaintop, and it was time to join them. The ancient removed the inner garment of knotted strips and wound it carefully around Treborra's shoulders.

"This is the history of the Jengg and all that came before," the ancient said. "Add to it the history of the Bachan. They are ended. Now a new tribe and a new history begin."

"What will we call our tribe? What colors will we wear?" Treborra asked.

The great figure was still for a time, then it said, "Be the tribe of the koomiok. Wear a single color, the white of the koomiok."

The last words of an ancient were of profound significance to Hult's people. Even so, these words startled the two hearers. No tribe had ever borne a single color before. But no tribe had ever sprung from Onhla of two worlds before, either. Nor had any other Onhla ever led a hunting pack of Insgar's white stalkers. These were new signs for a new race, and Hult found the ancient's words to his liking.

"We will be the Koomiok," he said.

"You brought me two pelts at the time of choosing. We will make new robes from them, in the color of our own tribe," Treborra suggested, and Hult agreed at once.

That night, as Treborra and Hult lay in one another's arms, the ancient left them. The mighty figure climbed the mountain to the high ledge where the others who had gone before sat with their faces turned to the darkness. It kindled the dreamfire and took its place beside the dreamers. There was no ceremony of departure. This was a time of fulfillment, not sadness.

In the morning, Treborra and Hult set to work making new robes for their return to Hraggellon. The ancient had left its gorwol cloak behind; Treborra rolled it carefully to preserve it for its destined use.

When the time came, Hult brought the pack to the far edge of the forest, and then released them. Several scuttled off at the chance, swift as shadows, glad for their release from the bondage this strange being had imposed upon them. Others hesitated, wavered, then moved off. Their departure was at first faltering and uncertain, but as they went farther from Hult, they moved ever faster.

Two remained, and would not leave their leader's feet. These two were the youngest, reaching barely to Hult's chest when they stood erect. They had been the first to give their allegiance, and they could not recant. Again he told them they were free, but they only lay still at his feet. He sensed a wordless hollow of loss and loneliness within them, and he hesitated; not from pity, but out of duty. The obligations of a leader to his pack were not taken lightly by an Onhla. If these koomiok wished to remain, he could not drive them off.

Treborra offered counsel. "If we take the name of the

koomiok, it would be right to have the creatures with us. They could hunt as well on Hraggellon," she said.

"The tormagon would attack them on sight."

"The tormagon would obey you. If you name these two our tribal beasts, nothing would dare attack them."

Hult knew that she was right. Treborra's advice was always sound. The thought of returning to the homeworld with new beasts, a new pack of their own, was a strong one.

"As you say. They come," he said.

The beasts understood. Their features were not made to express happiness, but their actions showed it. They rolled wildly in the snow, nipped at one another's snouts, and radiated a devotion that Hult experienced with a pleasure he had not known since his early days among the tormagons.

One of them came to Treborra and rubbed heavily against her leg, giving off a low rattling growl of pleasure. She plunged her fingers deep in its fur and scratched the rubbery skin. The other stalker, in a fit of sheer joy, cavorted in circles around Hult, sending sheets of snow in all directions.

"They must have names now," Treborra said.

"Name them, Treborra."

She thought for a moment, then said, "This one I name Jengg, and the other is Bachan."

They made their way to the river valley, avoiding the settlement of the fallen Onhla, and soon had passage on a downriver raft. The raftsmen were uncomfortable in the presence of two koomiok, even young ones, and uncertain what to make of a pair of large humanoids dressed in koomiok furs. But Hult paid them generously with furs of the burrowers, and the journey back to the *Grixlingen* was pleasant and untroubled. They arrived two days before the appointed time. Seb Dunan and his assistant arrived the next morning. The following day, the *Grixlingen* lifted off for Hraggellon.

The Hraggellian day/year, as observed in Norion, is equal to 244.6 days GSC. The complete annual cycle is referred to as a *dark*, or *darktime*. *Darktime* also refers to the extended period of darkness that constitutes this world's night/winter.

The cycle begins with *firstlight*, the appearance of the sun on the Brightside horizon. It is followed by *newlight*, the time of planting, and *harvest*. *Midlight* marks the noon/midsummer period of greatest heat, when the light penetrates most deeply into shadowlands, reaching the border of Starside. It is a time of potential drought. All cisterns and irrigation tanks are filled by early *midlight*, and the floodgates at the lower end of Lake Kariar are shut to preserve water for the next planting season. There is little activity in Norion during *midlight*.

Second planting and *second harvest* comprise afternoon/autumn. The floodgates are reopened and work is resumed. The day/year ends with *lastlight*. The floodgates are closed. The waterways freeze over. Darkness covers Norion, extending, in deepest *darktime*, from the downriver settlements through shadowlands into Starside. In 57.3 days GSC the cycle begins anew.

M. B. B. Bartolin, Primary

Third Hraggellian Contact Mission

VII.

HOME

Hult spent no time with the traders on the return voyage. He considered his business with them finished, and had no desire for human company. He had more pressing duties.

The koomiok required much care. They were restless and uneasy in the close confines of a driveship, and only Hult's continuous presence could calm them. Starfaring rations were skimpy and tasteless to them. Unless Hult was by, they would not eat.

Treborra could not help, for she had important duties of her own. From the ancient's cloak she fashioned a casing of gorwol fur to hold the histories of their old tribes. When this was done, she began to knot the story that was unfolding even as her fingers moved: the creation of the tribe of the Koomiok.

They worked on at their tasks, watch after watch, in an orderly little private world within the enclosure of the *Grixlingen*. Onhla, they lived as Onhla had always lived: apart. They ate and slept at their bodies' need, and obeyed no other commands. Long before the halfway watch had been reached, most of the crew had forgotten their presence aboard.

But Seb Dunan thought of them often. Things had gone badly for him since the landing on Insgar, and his mind turned ever more frequently to what the Onhla's furs could bring him. As the trip wore on, he grew almost desperate to see the alien pair. Four times he left his cabin to make his way through the *Grixlingen* to their remote quarters, and each time he turned back. He could not face that cold stranger in his current condition. He felt himself growing weaker with each watch that passed, and his determination waned with his strength.

Dunan had driven himself too hard, ignored too many warnings, and now he was paying the inevitable price. The scent-case had always provided strength and euphoria in moments of need, and he had come to rely on it more and more during this taxing mission. He had only deceived himself. Even the powerful inhalants mixed on Tarquin VII had their limitations, and he had gone beyond them. Two plus-gravity planets had been too much for his endurance. The pains in his chest had gotten severe during the stay on Insgar, and slowed him down badly. He trusted the scent-case to bring him through, and feared the meddling of ignorant healers. Even the *Grixlingen*'s medico was little more than a patcher and stitcher, sure to do more harm than good. Dunan wanted only to settle things, complete all the necessary arrangements, and then return to base and rest, his position secure for life. He was tired, and for the first time in his long life, afraid.

He sprawled in a narrow bunk, breathing shallow cautious breaths of the bland shipboard air and cursing his own folly. Making the rounds of those mining sites on Insgar was the finisher, he admitted to himself. That was when the pains got too bad to bear. Thought for a time I wouldn't get back to the *Grixlingen* alive.

Got to see the Onhla, he thought. No more of his evasions, I have to wring a firm promise of co-operation from him, and from his partner, too, she looks as good a hunter as he is, half-animal all of them, anyway. But better than those dog-faced Norionites. They'll bring in plenty of furs, that pair, and ask next to nothing in exchange. Those two things with them, ugly beasts, can't remember what they call them, but good thick furs, wouldn't mind adding them to the six but no, that wasn't the agreement. Have to stick to the agreement.

A dart of pain made him groan and start up. He fell back, his thoughts in a reeling muddle of ice and furs and clingers, of light-globes and scent-cases and cleansing plants and the

Saga of Daldirian and steep hillside paths and Remembrancers and the sight of a pale muscular humanoid with a
humped back swimming in the Moharil current like a child
frolicking in a puddle. He sank into unconsciousness for a
time and then came suddenly awake, possessed by a sense of
great urgency, his mind alert and clear.

Should tell the medico and have him put me in stasis, he
thought. But grief to him, I don't trust him. Nor the stasis
tank. Traveling across the galaxy frozen into an icicle, dead
as dead until some tech brings you back . . . if she can . . .
and if Command permits it. I'll take my chances awake.
Once I've finished my work. . . .

He pulled himself from the bunk and made his way unsteadily from the cabin. Waited too long, he told himself,
much too long. Only a dozen watches left until we reach
Hraggellon, and then they'll be gone and I'll never see them
again. Pain pricked his chest, but he ignored the warning.
He had to see the big tribesman. Time was short. He had to
see him now.

Dunan edged along the companionway, hands on the
bulkhead, moving slowly and with great effort. His forehead
was beaded, and drops of sweat trickled down his cheeks,
but he forced himself on. His legs grew weak under him,
and he stumbled but caught himself before falling. At a
junction he pushed himself from the supporting bulkhead
and found he could not make it to the other side. After two
staggering steps he collapsed and fell full length. An inferno
flared inside his chest. It was too late. He could barely move
or speak, and he knew he was close to death.

He lay helpless for a time, and then he tried to move. A
wave of pain wrenched his heart and tore a groan from him.
He gave up and lay still.

There was no more time, no time for the Onhla, no time
for anything. Should have had more sense, he thought. No
need to chase all over Insgar for trade goods, not with six
gorwol furs and a stock of light-globes aboard. And all those

plants. You had enough, he told himself angrily. You didn't need more. The pelts would have been enough. Now nothing can help. It's all over. Nothing can help. Nothing.

He clutched at the bulkhead. His hand shook, and closed on emptiness. "Nothing!" he gasped in a voice not his own, and then Seb Dunan died.

A crewman found the body two watches later and immediately summoned Clell Basedow. At first the young man was shocked. He did not want to believe that Dunan could have died so unexpectedly. He felt a sense of loss, for in his own narrow way, Clell had been fond of Dunan. The old trader had been gruff, and sometimes he was ill-tempered, but he knew his business better than anyone else Clell had ever known. It would be a long empty voyage back to the main base without him.

At that thought, the mood of the young apprentice changed. With Seb Dunan dead, he was in charge of the trading mission. He would take orders no more, for now, in an instant, he had arrived at equal footing with the captain. The mission had been a success; now it was his success and his triumph, solely his. He smiled, then burst into laughter; but in an instant he turned somber. He had duties and obligations now, things to attend to, decisions to make, work to do. No time for laughter. He had been given a great gift, but it was not enough merely to accept it, as a child would. He had to find a way to make this mission truly his, and show that he was not simply lucky. He summoned the ship's medico and after a brief report, left him with the body. He wanted to think on his future conduct of this mission, and plan it carefully.

When the *Grixlingen* locked into the landing ring on Hraggellon, Basedow's plan was firm. Seb Dunan had done much, but there was a way to do more. As the whine of the drivecoils died to silence, Basedow came to the Onhla's quarters accompanied by two armed security troopers.

Hult stepped from the compartment and saw the young trader standing before him, flanked by two much bigger men carrying long pistols. He knew at once that something was wrong, but he waited for the others to speak.

"We must talk, Onhla," the young man said.

"Why?"

"Things have changed since you saw us last."

"We had an agreement, the old trader and I. Agreements do not change," Hult said.

"The old trader is dead. There must be a new agreement," the young man said firmly.

Hult looked at him, then at the troopers, and said, "No."

"You don't seem to understand very well, Onhla, so listen to me carefully. You tricked old Dunan into taking you to another system for a mere six pelts. Well, he's dead now, and I'm in charge of this mission, and I'm not so easily duped. I intend to get proper payment for the use of a Sternverein ship," Basedow said.

Hult stood with his hands by his sides and made no reply. He understood this loud little man, and was thinking of how best to deal with him and his helpers. This was no time for talk. As he stood in thought, Treborra joined him and stood by his side. In her arms she carried the casing containing their tribal histories. At the sight of it, Basedow cried out and pointed to it accusingly. Treborra did not understand his words, but she drew back and clutched the casing tightly at this gesture.

"There's proof that you tricked us," Basedow said. "You kept gorwol furs for yourself, when you had promised them to us."

"I gave what I agreed to give."

"You held back. You said there weren't enough gorwol to give us more, but you took a pelt for yourself. That's thievery, Onhla, and it calls for punishment."

"This fur is not of Hraggellon. It was a gift from an ancient of the tribe of Jengg. He left it to us, to become a protection for the tribal histories," Hult said.

Basedow was silenced by the explanation, but only for a moment. He rallied quickly. He neither believed nor disbelieved what the Onhla said. It made no real difference to him. He knew what he wanted, and what he would have to do to achieve it.

"It doesn't matter where that fur came from. You tricked us, and you have to make up for it. I'm a fair man. I'm not asking anything unreasonable, just proper payment for all we've done. We've been gone very long, by Hraggellian time, and the gorwol have had time to multiply. You must bring us more furs. This many more," Basedow said, extending the fingers of both hands.

"When you next return to Hraggellon, I will bring that many gorwol pelts."

"We must have them now."

"Not now. Other things must be done."

"You'll get them now, Onhla, or your wife—your mate, or whatever she is—won't leave the ship." Clell gestured to the troopers, and they leveled their pistols at Hult's belly.

He had never seen the effect of a Sternverein shell on a human body, but he understood that these were weapons of great power. He did not move, and Clell went on, "Go and hunt. When you've brought back that many gorwol pelts, we'll release her. She'll be unharmed."

"You do wrong to violate an agreement."

"Don't talk to me of right and wrong, Onhla. You tried to outsmart the Sternverein, and you failed."

Hult ranged the koomiok stirring behind him. They sensed his alarm and anger, and obeyed his low growl of command. At the sound, Clell took a step back, closer to his guards.

"Don't try to frighten me, either. I'm not afraid of you. Snarling at me won't change things," he said.

The two troopers were at either side of Basedow, all three
bunched close together. The situation was right. Hult gave a
silent command. The two koomiok scuttled from behind
him, bellies low, and sprang upward, closing their jaws on
the pistol hands of the guards and using their weight to pull
the men off balance and bear them down. Hult lunged forward, seized Basedow by the throat, and flung him against
the bulkhead. He hit with a crack of bone and slid to the
deck, where he lay still. Hult took the pistols from the deck
and called off the koomiok. The men had resisted, and were
badly mauled, but they would survive. Hult dragged all
three into the compartment and secured them inside.

He and Treborra each took one of the weapons. They had
only a vague idea of how to use them, but it seemed wiser to
take them than to leave them behind. They made their way
to the main port without difficulty, and at the ramp were
greeted by one of the ship's officers.

"Did trader Basedow speak to you?" the officer asked.

"We discussed our agreement," Hult replied.

"Is he coming to the ramp to see you off?"

"No," Hult said.

The koomiok were growing impatient, and their impatience was of a sort to make the officer uneasy. He termi-
nated the conversation and stepped back to allow them to
depart. Without a backward glance, the tribe of Koomiok
left the *Grixlingen* to descend to the soil of their homeworld.

They had arrived late in the year. Second harvest was
over, and many workers and farmers had already returned
from the upriver settlements to take up their darktime quarters in Norion. The Onhla had no wish to enter the city.
They left the high road a short way from the spaceport and
cut across the hills to Lake Kariar.

It might be that the humans from the white ship would
pursue, at least until the fall of darkness. Hult thought it
best to take a hard trail. It would discourage pursuers, and
there would be small risk of meeting anyone. He stayed on

the mountainous side of the lake, where only mining camps were found. The miners were always among the first to return to Norion. He expected to meet no one on his way.

They crossed the Lesser Kariar, now little more than a stream, and proceeded to the River Kariar itself, at the upper bend of the lake. It, too, was near its low point; even so, it was a broad, deep river, and the koomiok had some difficulty in crossing. They were young yet, and their full strength lay before them. The waters of Insgar were all they knew, and the mildly flowing waters of Insgar had not prepared them for the rivers of Hraggellon. But they fought their way across, and Hult was pleased by their courage. They would do well on this world.

They circled the upper end of Lake Kariar until they came to the Upper Moharil. Its waters were already stilled. Hult led the way along the riverbank until they reached the point where the trail to Onhla lands led off on the opposite side. Here they camped and hunted until all the waters ceased to flow. They crossed the frozen river and with the dim afterglow of the sunken sun at their right hand, made their way past ranks of closed and shrunken sunseekers to home.

Hult had been advised of the time-dilating effect of drive-speed travel, but he paid no heed to the warning. If by human measurement much time had passed on Hraggellon during his absence, that did not concern him. The names assigned by humans to the changing positions of sun and stars and to the lengthening and shortening of shadows might be significant to human needs, but to an Onhla they were irrelevant. Hult's people lived by a different rhythm. Among the tribes, time was measured inwardly in ways no human could begin to understand.

But whether its passage be marked by human or Onhla measure, time is the record of change, and the darks that had come and gone on Hraggellon had wrought great changes. Hult and Treborra could ignore the changes and even deny that they had occurred; but they were not immune to their effects.

Orm the Peacebringer was now an aged tyrant, ruling Norion and the surrounding settlements with the capricious severity of unquestioned power. He had at last fulfilled the promise of his name. Peace reigned in Norion and the lands around, and not a single voice was heard in opposition. The Sixty Without Names had done their work conscientiously and well. The public guardians attended to lesser manifestations of discontent. All was orderly.

In all of Norion and the settlements, scarcely a Remembrancer was to be found. Long ago, just after the departure of the *Grixlingen* for Insgar, there had been an uprising in Norion at lastlight. That was always a restless time, when the city was swarming with returnees from upriver and downriver and the camps in the mountains, all of them carrying a lighttime's earnings and spending freely to insulate themselves against the long tedium of the approaching darktime. No one knew how the trouble started. It had been long since anyone dared to suggest the handiwork of the Sixty Without Names in its inception, but at the time, most believed them responsible. For many darks now, the custom had been to blame it all on an untimely outburst of memur. Whatever the cause, a quarrel broke out between a group of mineral traders and a pair of Remembrancers, young lildodes hired to witness and record a transaction. The details had long since been lost, as so many facts were now lost and forgotten. Rioting raged through lastlight and well into darktime, and when it finally grew quiet, the last Remembrancers in Norion were dead, victims of the anonymous brutality of a mob.

The rest of the Remembrancers, seeing the resentment growing against them under Orm's rule, had already fled to remote settlements. At the height of the riot, there were those who called for a mass expedition against the fugitives, one last drive to exterminate all trace of Orm's enemies and the enemies of the people of Norion. But the fear of being caught in the cold and dark of the Hraggellian night over-bore the hatred, and talk of pursuit died. When firstlight came, and all Norion poured outward to work the land, no Remembrancers were found.

They were not dead. From time to time after that, small bands were seen in the bleak lands close to the farthest shadowline, where humans did not long survive. The Re-membrancers had experienced human malevolence, and chose to risk the mindless cruelty of nature.

At first there were many small wandering groups, but as time passed their number dwindled. Some died in the rigors of darktime; others banded together for strength. As the number of bands grew less, so did the size of each. When Hult and Treborra returned to Hraggellon, only nine small groups of Remembrancers wandered in the cold country to darkward. But these survivors were a new kind of Remem-brancer.

They had learned to hunt, and to use the skins and furs of their quarry for protection against the bitter cold of dark-time. A life of flight and constant wariness hardened them, and to the strength of their minds they added strength and skill of the body. The arts they had for so long remembered and passed on to others they now strove to master for them-selves. They still felt the townsman's instinctive dread of the vast emptiness, his distaste for the long darkness and the bitter cold of the open lands, but they learned from experi-ence what measures could be taken. Slowly, painfully, at great cost, they learned to be survivors.

What the Remembrancers learned, the tormagon did not. Hult gave his old pack a way to survive, but ancient pat-terns held them too closely. The tormagons stayed in their old ways, followed the familiar trails, hunted the same grounds, and never returned to the island that might have become a rich new home. Two darks before the *Grixlingen* returned from Insgar, the last emaciated tormagon dropped in the mud on the trek to the firstlight hunting grounds and did not rise again.

Hult soon guessed what had happened, and his sorrow was mixed with anger. The tormagon had been shown the way and were too stupid to follow it, so they died. That was the rule of life in these hard lands. Now Hult would make his own pack from the beasts that ran beside him and Treborra. Life would go on. The Onhla would live again.

Hult and Treborra and the two stalkers, Jengg and Bachan, moved under the blaze of stars to their new hunting ground. Starside and the shadowlands were theirs, and they remained there apart, unseen by the humans of Norion or the fugitive Remembrancers, for many darks.

PART TWO: REMEMBRANCE

Section 6, further recommendations:

Since the fur trade has never materialized, and the profit on herbals and light-globes does not, in my judgment, justify their continuation in trade, I urge re-evaluation of our Hraggellian operation. Specifically, I recommend

a. That the next Hraggellian mission be assigned only to a Primary able and willing to work for the following objectives:

    i. unequivocal establishment of high-value local pelts as sole tender in all further commerce between Norion and the Sternverein;

    ii. thorough covert evaluation of the political situation in Norion; and

    iii. creation of a favorable climate for increased Sternverein presence in Norion;

b. That a full force of security troopers, and no other personnel, accompany the Primary; and

c. That unless the mission is completely successful, the Hraggellian trade be abandoned.

Morcon Gliss, Primary

Thirteenth Hraggellian

VIII.

RETURN TO HRAGGELLON

Orm the Peacebringer died at a great age, and his son Orm the Builder succeeded him almost without incident. The second Orm was in his middle years when he came to power, and he felt a great sense of urgency. It seemed to him that he had been allotted an unfairly short span in which to exercise his abilities. Accordingly, he worked at a furious pace and forced Norion to work with him.

The city was expanded, and all its storage facilities increased. The great sheltering dome was raised even higher and strengthened fivefold. With the help of machinery brought by the white ships that landed every several darks, a degree of comfort unknown to past generations became commonplace. While Norion was not transformed into a paradise, it was nevertheless much improved: the air was heated and circulated more efficiently; the arcades and walks were kept clean and free of stench; outbursts of memur were less frequent, and when they did occur, less extreme.

A fine new road was built joining the landing rings and the city. The floodgates were much improved, and the quays were rebuilt and increased in number. Nothing at all was done for the settlements downriver, or beyond Lake Kariar. They were unimportant to Orm the Builder. Only Norion mattered. He wished to leave behind him a city fit for a ruler's dwelling; he could spare no time or energy for refurbishing work camps.

When he died in an unfortunate accident, there followed a bloody interregnum, a time of great uncertainty. Eventually his youngest son became ruler of Norion and all Hraggellon, and took the title of Orm the Benefactor. The epithet was considerably narrower in application than those claimed by his forebears, for while the first Orm had brought peace, at a bloody price, and the second of that name had indeed been an insatiable builder, the third Orm had, by the twelfth dark of his reign, benefited no one but himself.

He lacked not energy, but direction. With no remaining enemies worth fighting and nothing left to build, he spent his time sporting, drinking, and siring strong, ugly children on a succession of partners. His life was like that of the old rulers, and he was not happy with it. He believed that he was capable of some great deed, but could not discover what that deed might be. And so he went on from dark to dark, the crafty mind in his brute's body growing ever more frustrated.

And then a white ship came, bearing a special emissary of the Sternverein as Mission Primary. This was the first ship to land since his accession, and Orm decided to receive the emissary and his party in state. He was still planning the ceremony when the emissary arrived alone at the royal residence and requested audience.

Orm was taken aback by such bold directness. These things were not done in Norion. He felt a faint whisper of uneasiness; here was a starfarer, one who had walked on other worlds and seen their wonders, one for whom Norion, with all its splendor, did not mark the beginning and end of human accomplishments: one who would not be impressed by Orm, or his predecessors, or their works. For just a moment, Norion seemed a shabby place, and Orm could imagine the stranger looking on it with a tolerant smile, praising it in bland and meaningless phrases, and moving on to laugh at this world and its ruler when among other starfarers. Orm did not permit laughter at his expense. A low involuntary growl escaped him at the thought.

But his mood changed quickly. Let the emissary do and think what he would, Hraggellon had things the Sternverein wanted, and could get nowhere else. They had no choice but to treat its ruler with respect. He gave word for the emissary to be admitted, and sat forward on his raised bench, his big hands bunched on his thick thighs, elbows out, in an aggressive posture, while the man approached.

Orm was impressed, and did his best to conceal it. The starfarer was tall—taller than most Hraggellians, tall even for an otherworlder—and dressed in a somber black uniform with a silver-trimmed black cloak over his shoulders. His black boots gleamed. His short black hair was touched with silver, but he did not appear to be much past his youth, and in fine physical condition.

Most striking of all was the emissary's posture, as stiff and straight as an icicle. At the foot of Orm's dais he bowed from the waist, then stood erect, silent, looking steadily at the ruler of Norion. Orm saw a darkness behind those eyes that unnerved him. He waved the emissary to a bench at his right hand.

"You are most welcome to Norion, Primary. I had hoped to entertain you and your party before your departure," Orm said. "I would have sent word, but now I can invite you myself."

"Orm is most kind," his visitor replied.

"I think it's good for us to learn more about one another. The Sternverein have helped Hraggellon, and we've provided them with valuable goods for their trade on other worlds. Perhaps we can find new ways to profit each other. Perhaps we have other goods to trade."

"We had hoped to discuss the trade agreement with the Benefactor," the emissary said.

"Good. Very good. I look forward to that."

"We had also hoped to remain on Hraggellon longer than the earlier ships have done, if the Benefactor will permit us."

"Stay as long as you like," Orm said expansively. Noticing the visitor's rigid posture, he added, "I see you find our benches uncomfortable. They're not built for creatures without padding on their bones. You have my permission to stand, or to sit elsewhere, if you wish."

"It is not the fault of these excellent benches, Benefactor. My back was broken long ago. I wear a device to support it."

Orm twitched an ear and shook his head in sympathy. "You starfaring folk lead dangerous lives. Though for that matter, my father died the same way, broken back, and he never left Norion. He was inspecting the dome, and he fell."

"A pity," his visitor murmured.

"What pity? It brought me to the rule," Orm said sharply.

"I only meant that it is an unfortunate way for a ruler to die."

"I don't know any fortunate ways. Do you?"

"None, Benefactor."

"Well, then," Orm said, and fell silent.

Orm had never learned to be self-effacing, and the habit of absolute power made it difficult for him to feel insecure; nonetheless, he found himself ill at ease in the company of this black-clad otherworlder. The fellow was respectful, soft-spoken, exhibiting all the proper deference to a planetary ruler; but even his submissiveness was aloof and superior. Orm did not like having him here, and resented his intrusion. He did not want to dismiss him too quickly, lest he leave convinced that the Benefactor of Norion was a speechless boor; but Orm could think of no more to say, not now, not without consulting his Remembrancers and learning more about the Sternverein agreements.

He had no wish to pass the time exchanging idle remarks. Polite talk was not a gift of his people. The emissary was eying the motion painting that covered one wall of Orm's chamber and sniffing—rather too foppishly, Orm thought—at a Tarquinian scent-case on his left wrist. He turned, and Orm waited for him to speak.

"A restful scene, Benefactor. A gift from the Sternverein?" the visitor asked.

"The Sternverein gives us no gifts. We traded two ship-loads of Tears of Yadd for that ocean scene," Orm informed him.

"About the trade goods, Benefactor. . . ."

"What about them? Speak freely," Orm said, glad for the chance to let the visitor reveal something of himself.

"The light-globes remain useful to us and popular on some of the remoter worlds. We would continue to trade in them; perhaps at a slightly reduced level. In exchange, we can offer improved cold-climate equipment that will make Starside more accessible to your people."

"My people don't need Starside. They have Norion."

"There might be great wealth in Starside."

Orm laughed. "Ice and wind is all you'll find in Starside. If that's wealth, Hraggellon is the richest world in the galaxy."

"There is other wealth. Fine furs, for instance, are much desired on worlds where no fur-bearing creatures live," the emissary said.

"Not many fur-bearing creatures left on this world, either. Maybe none at all, now. I haven't seen a new-caught pelt since before I came to rule. The tormagon are all dead. The gorwol have been extinct since before I was born."

"Perhaps not, Benefactor," the visitor said mildly.

"What do you mean, 'perhaps not'? Do you think you know more about Hraggellon than I do?"

"I know a different Hraggellon. I was here long ago, in the time of the Peacebringer, when the trade agreement was reached. I spoke with the Peacebringer himself."

Orm glared in frank disbelief at the pale unwrinkled face of the man beside him. "The Peacebringer is long dead after ruling for many darks, and the trade agreement came early in his rule. You look scarcely older than I am."

"Space travel has a strange effect on the passage of time, Benefactor. By the Galactic Standard Calendar, I am a very old man—far beyond the longest lifetime of my race. But my physical age is scarcely past youth."

"You're either old or young. You can't be both at the same time. How do you explain it?" Orm demanded.

"The explanation is too complicated for my understanding," the emissary said humbly. "It is said that only a score of men in all the galaxy understand it fully. I simply know it happens, as the dark and light come to Norion whether or not one understands why."

Orm grunted and looked dubious. "Never mind light and dark. I don't like this business of being old and young all at once. It's not natural." He was thoughtful for a moment, then he turned to his visitor and asked, "What was the Peacebringer like? Did you know him well?"

"I spoke with him only once, but I saw him often. He was immensely powerful, much like the Benefactor in frame. His strength was amazing."

"So is mine. Everyone knows that. Did you see the Builder, too?"

"He was not yet born."

"Not yet . . . ? He was old when he died, and you . . . how could you . . . ?" Orm was greatly perturbed.

"As I said, space travel causes time to pass in a strange way for starfarers."

Orm edged away from the visitor. He had heard his father mention this paradox once, and had always considered it a tale, something made up simply to confuse children. Such things made no sense. One grew older, or else one died. No one could live as long as these starfarers were said to live, watching generations pass while they themselves aged only a little. It was not natural. It was not fair. Orm brooded on the thought for a time, and came to a conclusion: if anyone should enjoy long life, it should be rulers. It should be Orm.

"We must talk about this further," he said.

"As the Benefactor desires. Our ship is at your service, our goods are ready for your inspection, and our troopers will assist in any way they can."

"Good. Good." Orm responded moodily.

Again there was a brief silence, and then the emissary said, "We had begun to discuss the trade agreement, I believe."

"Yes. I can tell you this: we have a new source of Tears of Yadd. We'll be able to supply many more than we ever have before. And in return we want machines to help us raise more food, and nutrients for the soil."

"We can supply your wants. But you must supply ours."

"What do you want?"

"There is interest in fine furs on some of the worlds we deal with, and Hraggellon is the home of the finest and rarest of fur-bearing animals, the gorwol."

"It was," Orm corrected him.

"Some think it may still be," the emissary said.

"Who thinks this? Some fools who have never seen Hraggellon and know nothing about it?" Orm said scornfully. "Men on some overheated world, who deal with talk and soundscriber reports and other people's ideas?"

"No, Benefactor. I, for one, believe that even now, Onhla still live deep in Starside and hunt the gorwol."

"You believe nonsense. Their hunting packs are all dead. Not even an Onhla can survive without a hunting pack."

"They have hunting packs. White beasts from another world, a place called Insgar."

Orm pondered this news. The man in black was proving to be much more than he had first appeared—ageless, full of unsuspected knowledge. There might be much to be gained from him. But Orm did not wish to appear overeager. "I find this hard to believe," he said. "In all my life, no one has seen an Onhla. They are said to have died in a great plague long ago, before the time of the Peacebringer."

"I have seen Onhla," said the emissary.

"Here? On Hraggellon? When?" Orm demanded.

"It was long ago, but there were two Onhla, a male and a female, partnered. They headed for Starside with a pair of white beasts. No one has seen them since, or heard of them, but I believe they live there still. By now, there might be many more of them."

Orm was angered by this revelation. "And why do you know of this when I do not? Why was I not informed at once?"

"You were not yet born, Benefactor. And those who knew were badly injured and could not speak or travel for a long time."

"So . . . Onhla live and hunt in Starside."

"I believe so."

"And have been there since the time of the Peacebringer." Orm weighed the implications of this fact and said, "They must have many furs."

"Very likely. And the Sternverein would trade generously for gorwol pelts."

"Pelts were not part of the original agreement. Peacebringer agreed to trade Tears of Yadd and certain plants, but not furs," Orm said. "I am no lildode, but I remember that much."

"Perhaps we should reach a new agreement," the emissary suggested.

"Perhaps. Are you empowered to make one?"

"I am head of the most powerful family in the Sternverein and a respected trader. It was I who persuaded them to trade for rendrood and Tears of Yadd. On this mission, I am Mission Primary, unassisted. When I speak, I speak for the Sternverein, and no one will question an agreement I make."

"Good. First, though, we must hear the old agreement. I'll have food brought in, and send for my lildodes."

For the first time, the man in black showed mild surprise at Orm's words. "Lildodes, Benefactor? I had heard that all Remembrancers were either slain or banished from Norion by order of the Peacebringer."

"A few were kept. For the royal convenience."

"Surely our soundscribers are more accurate, Benefactor.

If not, I will see that better ones are made expressly for Norion."

"The soundscribers are good," Orm said, enjoying his momentary ascendancy over the visitor. "They satisfy me. I retain the lildodes simply as a useful tool. They were always the most practical order of Remembrancers. Their memories caused no unrest. But the others . . . constantly reminding the people of things dead and gone, and best forgotten. Enough if my people remember their agreements and their ruler. They need no Remembrancers."

"Indeed not, Benefactor. That was the thought of the Peacebringer when he drove them out. Are all the others gone, then?"

"They're gone from Norion. A few still wander in the far reaches. Some, it is said, have even ventured into Starside."

"The Benefactor allows them to live?"

Orm sniffed and twitched an ear casually. "They have been banished, and are no longer under my protection. That's punishment enough. They live until I feel a need to eliminate them."

His visitor nodded. After a thoughtful pause he said, "And yet out there, far from watchful eyes, they might be planning . . . not that anyone would dare to rise against the Benefactor, of course, but if the evodes spread the ancient myths, and the paturdodes recall to others the old laws and customs. . . ."

"What do you mean? Do you think those weaklings might be a danger to me?"

"Who would dare to threaten the Benefactor? Besides, they must be dying out. A handful of Remembrancers can threaten no one."

Orm's voice was hard. "Remembrancers are not the only ones who went into exile. There are those who disliked the Peacebringer's rule, and the Builder's, and even a few who would oppose mine. Not many. But they are not dying out. Not any longer. Some have survived since the Peacebringer's time, and if any folk last that long beyond Lake Kariar, they don't die out easily."

"Perhaps not. But I am presumptuous to speak of Hraggellian matters to the Benefactor. I should confine my words to trade," the visitor said.

Orm grunted assent and summoned his Remembrancers. He was annoyed and disturbed by this starfarer's words. Was it possible that a few wandering bands of fugitives, struggling to keep a little life going in the cold wastes, could constitute a danger to Orm the Benefactor? It seemed absurd even to contemplate. And yet rulers were overthrown, dynasties toppled, and often from unsuspected causes. He had heard of such things.

This starfarer had brought new concerns with him. But he had brought the promise of great things, too. Orm thought of the possibilities.

A ruler who never grew old would be more powerful than any who had ever held sway on Hraggellon. He would not have to destroy enemies—he could outwait them. Time, the most powerful weapon of all, would be his, if he learned to use the power of the driveships.

On the other hand, it was always well to destroy one's enemies when one could. A simple expedition—a hunting party, leaving at firstlight—and it could all be over. Everyone would know that there was no way of fleeing Orm the Benefactor. It might be a wise move; or it might not. Orm frowned. This was a decision that would require much thought.

While Orm brooded, his visitor sat quite content. Now a high Sternverein official, Clell Basedow had long anticipated his return to Hraggellon. He had been here only a short time, but already he had the foretaste of success for this mission.

Orm could be handled easily enough, no doubt about that. He was stupid, vain, suspicious—the perfect foil. He was already obviously thinking of the danger posed by the

Remembrancers; action was sure to follow, and the Sternverein would gladly offer assistance. Once in Starside, a
force of Sternverein troopers would hunt down the Onhla
and put their supply of gorwol pelts into the proper hands.
The troopers would have no trouble with the surviving Remembrancers. Orm would be in the grip of the Sternverein
for the rest of his reign, and Hraggellon would be in their
power. Everything fell into place neatly and simply.

Clell's only regret was that so much time had passed before his return; not for him, since he had been in space, but
for Hraggellon. That hulking tribesman who had snapped
his back like a stick could not still be living. Onhla were said
to be long-lived, but not miraculously so. It was too much to
hope for.

The Remembrancers entered on silent feet and bowed
low to their ruler. Clell rose, erect and straight, towering
over the squat Hraggellians, and took a place at the foot of
the dais where his human height was less obvious. At Orm's
command, the lildodes began to recite in unison, in the practiced monotones of their vocation. A dreary people, Clell
thought, raising his scent-case; husks of past life; relics;
dead things; and quite unnecessary. He still had old Seb
Dunan's soundscriber record of the original agreement.

The droning voices set Clell's thoughts to wandering. His
enemy was surely dead by now, but he might be punished
still. Any Onhla on this world would be descended from that
nameless brute's line. He had violated a treaty with the
Sternverein, caused permanent injury to three of its
members, and probably contributed in some underhanded
way to the death of old Dunan. Someone would pay for
that. His descendants would suffer in return for Clell's long
agony and helplessness, and would pay in full. What plague
could not accomplish, Clell Basedow would do. The Onhla
would soon be extinct at last.

In this non-literate society, business transactions are conducted before Truespeakers . . . a minor order of a caste known as Remembrancers who . . . serve as the collective living record of Hraggellian civilization. Certain groups of Remembrancers devote their powers of memory to business, others to formulas and medical lore . . . the most honored and respected, to the Saga of Daldirian and related matter. . . .

By law, no Remembrancer can ever plead forgetfulness. They do not carry arms, and remain apart from the incessant power struggles of Norion. Their allegiance is to absolute fidelity to fact. . . .

Remembrancers . . . use no facial expressions or gestures when reciting a memory. They are trained from childhood to . . . avoid intrusion of self into content. To distort meaning, to add or drop a single syllable, is a disgrace. To lie is the one unpardonable offense.

Eno Glaser, Tertiary
Second Hraggellon Contact Mission

IX.

SECOND FLIGHT

The Remembrancers had learned caution. For safety, they remained far distant from one another and never came together. A tenuous contact was maintained by the couriers who made the dangerous journeys between the scattered bands.

Some had settled in the tundras beyond the Pinjanari Mountains, on the ocean shore. They were the smallest group, remnants of a band that had risked crossing the wild waters to seek lands said to lie beyond. The seafarers were never heard of afterward.

The second band had wandered far into Brightside, to the foot of the Ravagund Hills, where a cold ocean current kept the temperature and humidity at a bearable level despite the eternal sunlight. The third group had gone deep into the shadowlands to settle at the foot of the black lake that bordered the Onhla hunting grounds.

The leader of this group was a woman named Shaelecc. In all the long history of the Remembrancers, governance and policy had been in the hands of the females, while the males devoted themselves to the work of memorization from childhood on. Under the rigors of long wandering, this structure had proven disastrous, and Shaelecc, once in command, had changed it. The duty of remembrance she had placed second to the duty of survival. Now the females shared in the work of memory and the males took a greater part in the daily concerns of the tribe.

There were mutterings and whispers when Shaelecc first announced the change, but great praise for her wisdom when it proved successful. The band mastered the ways of the cold country and began to grow in strength and number.

Now Shaelecc was growing old. Her husband and chief

adviser, Syger, was older. But their band was strong and confident, and showed promise of surviving.

For many darks, their home was the campground by the lake. The bleak and unrelenting cold of the first darks spent here had claimed many lives; but children were born to take the place of the lost elders, and the young were strong. They grew up in the ways of the cold country and feared it less. The memories of dead tribes and lost expeditions, of tracking and hunting in the white wastes, of food-gathering in the brief lighttimes, of wind and weather and safe terrain, now became their precious tools of survival. No longer were such memories held in the minds of mendodes and varasdodes, stored against the needs of others; now they were of common application and daily use.

Even as some memories grew more valuable, others became of little use, and were forgotten. Agreements made by others were no longer the concern of the Remembrancers; those who would have become lildodes, memorizing contracts and traders' pacts, now learned to hunt. The paturdodes, who once held in their memories all the history of Hraggellon back to the time when the first tormagons stood erect and left the dark lands to live as humans, now learned the ways of the land, and its bounty. Only the evodes lived on unchanged, preserving the myths and legends of their people, and certain gifted youths were marked from an early age as future evodes and looked upon with respectful envy by peers and elders alike. The evodes were the life of the Remembrancers. Other memories could be discarded, but while one evode lived, all lived.

A second generation of exiles grew to maturity in the campground by the black lake, and as their number grew, their hunting grounds extended. Others, fugitives from the cruelty of the Orm dynasty, joined them. Some of the young hunters even dared to venture into Starside, but few went deep, and despite their caution, not all returned. They spread laterally through shadowlands, into the fringes of the old Onhla territory. Some were fearful at this incursion. The Onhla, they said, were barbaric creatures and might do them harm if they suspected an invasion.

The young hunters scoffed at such fears. The Onhla were long dead, as everyone knew. And besides, said these strong, confident youths, the people need not fear Onhla or anyone else. Their hunters will protect them.

No Onhla appeared. The settlement by the dark water grew and prospered, and the generations that had not known Norion agreed that whatever had brought them here was no misfortune.

The bad news came as darktime was ending. Firstlight had already come to Norion, and the yearly exodus of workers was beginning. With the workers came news of the city's doings, and word from the other Remembrancers' camps.

The courier from the Pinjanari Remembrancers told of an expedition being mounted in Norion. He had not dared to approach the city or the settlements too closely, or reveal his interest too plainly, but he had heard many of the upriver travelers refer to the expedition as punitive in nature. He stayed to learn no more. The ruler of Norion had no interest in punishing anyone but the Remembrancers and their friends.

The courier arrived, weak from exhaustion, while the Brightside horizon was still only a pale line of light. Upon hearing his message, Shaelecc assembled her council in the dwelling cave and had the courier repeat his full report to them. She then dismissed him and bade the others speak.

"He tells us little, and we must make important decisions," one of the men said. "How big is this expedition, and when does it leave? Can we be certain it is meant for us?"

"So many darks have passed since the flight, and Orm is long dead. Can they still hate us?" another asked.

"We never learned why they turned on our fathers so

suddenly. Until we know that, we cannot expect to know if they have stopped hating us. Until we know we are safe, we must be cautious," Shaelecc replied.

"True, we must be cautious," they agreed.

"Do the lildodes in Norion send any message?" Syger asked.

"They side with the oppressor now. We can think of them as friends no longer. We must be cautious, I say again."

"But how cautious? Are we safe here, or must we go elsewhere?"

"I think we can move no deeper into Starside. Here, we can hunt and even grow food during midlight. Only one planting, but it suffices for our needs. Nothing grows in Starside. The creatures dwelling there must travel constantly in search of food. We would have to follow them or die," Shaelecc said. "We would have to learn to be nomads. Can we change our way of life again, and still survive?"

They considered the question, debated it at length, and at last decided that they could move no farther into the darkness without too great risk. One of the females then suggested that they travel to Brightside and join the Remembrancers who lived at land's end, beyond the Ravagund Hills. The prospect of year-round light and warmth was tempting, and many favored this course of action.

"As Daldirian and Redmayne increased their strength tenfold by joining magic to the force of arms, so we would become stronger by union with those to Brightside," Syger declared.

"Greater strength might also prove a danger," one of the evodes pointed out. When the paradox was questioned, he explained, "The saga itself warns us of such a thing. Be it remembered, in the passage of the hunt on the burning field, spoken by Daldirian himself:

'When foeman flees alone,
Forbear to lift the sword.

But when upon the wind
The footbeats of a horde
Make promise of a clash
With glory as reward,
Then raise the eager blade
And face a worthy contest undismayed.'"

The others listened in silence to the flat monotone of the old evode's reciting voice. Several murmured, "Be it so remembered." The message was clear.

"Another consideration," said one of the females. "No courier has come from the Ravagund band since before the last dark. They may have fled elsewhere."

"Or died of hunger, or been massacred," Shaelecc added.

"Have we no way of learning the true purpose of this expedition—if, indeed, it is real and not just a rumor? During darktime, strange tales are born in Norion. This may be no more than an idle story," one male said.

"We have no spies in Norion, none in the settlements. Orm's soldiers destroyed all, or bought their loyalty," Shaelecc reminded him.

"But Orm died in the Dark of the Long Skyblaze. His son ignored us. Why would his son's son resume the persecution?"

"I say again, we do not know why it began, or why it stopped so suddenly, so we can never be certain when it may begin again. We can only be cautious."

"Then we must move on," Syger said. "The only way is into Starside, but we need not stay. There may be something beyond Starside—a safe haven no one has ever reached before."

A woman rose to speak. "We are not Onhla. True, we have learned much about surviving, but the cold and darkness of Starside are unending. Nothing can live there for long. We would be wandering aimlessly through unknown lands. It would mean exposing ourselves to great danger."

"Danger to stay. Danger to join the other bands. Danger to move deeper into Starside. We have small choice," Syger said.

"We cannot be sure about the dangers of Starside. The evodes have many legends and tales of the cold and emptiness, and of strange creatures unlike those that know the light. But the varasdodes, who know all races, have no memories to give us. Perhaps we fear imaginary dangers," a man pointed out.

"Freezing and starving are not imaginary. Many Remembrancers learned that in the first darks of exile," the woman responded.

"The first darks of exile are far behind us. We have learned much. Our hunters go into Starside now, and return safely."

"Not all return."

"That is true. But hunting is always dangerous."

A silence descended on the group as all thought on the problem. After a time Syger spoke, his voice low and tentative. "If we were to wait until the shadowline has receded to its farthest point, we could explore with the least danger. Be it remembered, this was done in the time of Marnon, in the Dark of the Long Hunger, when a great force of trappers was sent from Norion to take supplies for the next dark."

"And none returned. All perished in the cold."

"They were unprepared and had far to go. We are close to Starside, and would prepare well."

Shaelecc expanded this thought, after pondering it for a while. "A small band of the best hunters could prepare themselves for the worst cold and follow the shadowline into Starside. If they leave caches of food and fuel behind, the rest of us can follow safely. We can push deeper into the dark than any but the Onhla have gone."

"But why? What does Starside offer but cold and darkness and a lonely death?" one man asked.

"We might come to the edge of Hraggellon, and fall into nothingness!"

"Be it remembered—Vulo offered proofs that Hraggellon is round, not flat, and if it is round, then there is hope for us," said Syger.

"But Shotol offered proof that it is flat!"

Another voice spoke up. "Perhaps Syger is right, and there is another land—a better land—beyond Starside. The ice must end somewhere."

"It might end so far away that we can never reach it. And if we should, who knows what dangers we might find? We might learn that there are worse tyrants than Orm," the first speaker said. Another, supporting him, said, "We all remember the tales of Wuran the Defiler."

"We remember other tales, as well," Syger countered. "The fragments from before the Forgotten Darks that have always been treated as legend—they offer hope."

"Legends can kill. They are not memories, to be trusted. They are wishes. Our brothers believed the legends that spoke of traveling on the water as easily as one travels on land, and now they are lost," the man said.

"Perhaps not. We travel on the inland waters with ease; there may be a way to cross the outer waters safely. Our brothers may have found a better land and even now await us there."

A woman rose and the others fell silent. She was Jeesha, second only to Shaelecc in age and authority. She spoke seldom, but her words were always heeded. Now her voice was solemn.

"I hear much that disturbs me and frightens me," she began. "One speaks of wandering into ice and darkness, another says we must cast ourselves into the sea. The old wisdom is being discarded as if it had no meaning. All this because a messenger comes with a rumor from Norion."

"We must be cautious," Shaelecc said.

"We must be reasonable," Jeesha countered. "We must first know the truth, and only then—"

A great uproar arose at the cave entrance. As the elders stirred uneasily, a hunter burst in upon them. "One of the Ravagund band!" he cried. "He comes alone, injured—you must hear him!"

"Bring him," Shaelecc said.

The messenger was scarcely more than a boy. He was bundled in layers of light, bright-colored clothing and his hands and feet were swathed in wrappings. As they laid him by the fire and a mendode skilled in healing began to examine his wounds, Shaelecc and the others marveled at the deep color of his skin, so different from the pallor of their own. They had heard that the unending light of Brightside did such things, but even so, the sight of a Remembrancer so changed surprised them, and a few were troubled. They thought of Jeesha's words. Too much was changing. In all this changing, something was sure to be lost.

The boy's injuries were not severe, but he was exhausted and starving. He gulped water and tried to swallow food, but his stomach rejected it all. The healer brewed a strengthening herbal drink, and the boy sipped it slowly and retained it. He was silent as his injuries were cleaned and dressed, then he burst into a wild stream of disjointed fragments.

Words poured from him. His voice rose and fell, and often it vibrated and cracked with strong emotion. The evodes looked uncomfortably at one another, avoiding the youth's eyes. They could conceive of no circumstance that could force them to lose control so completely and shamefully. Such a change as they now saw was far more disturbing than a shading of the skin. In changes of this kind lay the destruction of the Remembrancers. The elders thought this, but remained silent out of pity.

The youth cried out loudly, tried to rise, and collapsed.

The mendode attending him covered him carefully and moved him near the fire. He would sleep for a long time.

When he awoke, he was calm. He ate a light meal, drank more of the healing herbal broth, and was given clothing more suited to this climate than the garments in which he had traveled.

There was some difficulty in finding clothing to fit him. The robes of all the others were too large for his frame. He was not stocky and thick-set, like those of the cold country, but slender, slightly taller, and muscular, lacking the insulating fat that lay beneath their smooth, pale skins. To the young hunters, he looked like a starveling, and his quick recovery impressed them.

After a second sleep and a full meal, he met with the elders once again. He was in control of his voice and his feelings now, and spoke in a monotone, reciting facts and observations with total objectivity, as a Remembrancer must. But the strain on him was obvious. He recited no ancient memories, cushioned by time and anonymity into bland history. These were his own experiences, as raw and painful as the wounds on his body. And whatever small reassurance his voice might offer them, the story he told was cause for fear.

"The question of leaving our settlement on the coastal plain was first raised five darks ago, because of the natural dangers and hardships of our surroundings," he began. "The soil was rich, and we grew food in abundance, but crops were uncertain because of the storms that sweep the coast and destroy the plantings. These storms were unlike any in our memory. I have seen homes lifted from the ground and blown into the sea by the chedgorn that comes down the coast without warning. The river was full of good fish to eat, but the current was very strong. Since our settling there, twenty-one rafts were drawn past the barrier and swept into the ocean. No one ever escaped that current. For these reasons, many felt that we should seek a new home. Others were willing to accept the dangers we knew rather than to attempt a new life that might be no better. After six councils and long debate, no decision had been reached. Then, as darktime was ending, we learned of a plan being laid in Norion against the Remembrancers. We could obtain no details, only the word that an expedition would leave with the light to seek out and destroy us all. Council was convened at once, and it was judged that the greatest safety lay in union with our fellow Remembrancers in shadowlands."

He paused for questions. When none came, he went on in the same level voice. "To keep our flight secret, it was judged that we would cross the strait and travel through the empty land beyond, until we were past the settlements of the men from Norion. It was a hazardous crossing, and we lost six rafts, but all judged it necessary and right. The way was hard, but we met no one other than those who sold us their beasts."

An elder had signaled for a question, and the speaker paused and touched lips and ear lobe.

"Two questions," said the evode. "First, how could you cross the strait and survive? There are no memories of such a feat."

"A mendode calculated that we could cross safely if we had strong lines to guide us. The first four rafts to attempt the crossing were lost, but the fifth brought a line across. We used the first line to draw others. Once we had the lines firmly fixed, it took only strength to make the crossings. All but two were able to do it. One was struck by a floating log and knocked adrift. The other was lost for reasons we do not know."

"My second question is this: if you made the crossing safely, and met no one, what became of the others? Proceed."

The youth breathed deeply, composed himself to respond, and said, "We traveled up the River Vensariar and reached Lake Durvensar ahead of the light. The waters were still frozen. It was judged that we would camp on the ice and renew our provisions before moving on. When we awoke, the lildodes began to drill work holes in the ice. I went alone to attend the animals. Suddenly there was a vibrating of the ice all around us. Some said it was breaking, but we knew that the ice breaks only with the coming of light. A noise came to us, like the sound of a chedgorn rolling near. It was dark, and we could not see, our eyes were not accustomed. Fear swept us, and people ran about aimlessly, picking up their goods, throwing them down again, crying out to one another. I have not seen such a sight as this, ever before. . . ." He paused again, for a time, and all present understood that he was not awaiting questions but taking time to master himself. He braced his shoulders, looked up, and continued. "We saw a cloud approaching us along the ice. The noise grew and the ice shook beneath our feet. I mounted one of the haxopods, thinking to ride to higher ground and study the storm, for I believed it to be a storm. It was not. In the cloud rode a force of men, and they rode through the camp killing everyone in sight. All were slain, and their goods were scattered. I will say no more. When the attackers saw me, I fled. They pursued and wounded me, but I escaped."

Came the question, "Were the attackers men of Norion?"

"I cannot say with certainty. They wore garments unknown to memory. But I believe many were from Norion, from the way they rode. There were others riding with them, men dressed in black. Otherworlders."

"Did they pursue long?"

"Yes. I tried to lead them off. I believe they do not know where I went," the youth said.

No further questions came. The youth was conducted from the council to a place of rest. When he had left, Shaelecc spoke. "They come to destroy us, and they bring with them otherworlders. They have weapons unknown to memory and beyond our imagining. We cannot stand against them. We will go to Starside."

No one dissented. A few of the young hunters mumbled about standing their ground and fighting, but they went with the rest.

The Remembrancers, once decided, moved swiftly. The camp was dismantled, the haxopods loaded, and all was ready for departure before a meal was taken. After eating, they turned their backs on the skyblaze, those shimmering curtains of light that had begun to flicker and dance about the Brightside horizon, and headed into darkness and the unknown.

. . . unable to find definite proof that this phase, variously called *nithboorg, neethborg,* or *nithbrog,* actually occurs. All accounts speak of extreme physical change and mental alteration, amounting almost to mutation into a new species. [Mission Bio-historian Stennsen believes that the concept is a racial memory of some early unsuccessful stage in the physical evolution of Hraggellian humanoid life, transferred to the Onhla.]

Not one Onhla in the *nithboorg* phase has been seen by a trustworthy observer. This is explained by citing their preference for the darkness and solitude of deep Starside, where they meditate and commune with the spirits of past generations.

Having studied all available evidence, we must judge this aspect of Onhla lore to be pure legend. For a primitive race of nomadic hunters to develop into the kind of creature these legends describe is culturally impossible. It is obviously an immortality fantasy. *There is no third stage of Onhla life.* Most probably, some rare Starside creature of roughly humanoid appearance is being identified as an Onhla life-phase through simple extrapolation of their known metamorphosis into the reproductive stage.
[Analogues: the Mu'ure of Prodengaria; the Yeti of Old Earth; the oceanic Thagwondis of 3-Lathpen-267.]

Soman Wirsing, Secondary

Fourth Hraggellon Contact Mission

X.

SECOND ENDING

The koomiok raced ahead, their flat white forms rippling over the frozen ground of Starside. They were young and full of energy, and their leaping and frisking was good to see.

When they vanished from sight, Hult ranged them; but he withheld his mental reins and let them run free. No enemies lived here, and the koomiok knew the signs of danger in their surroundings. He felt no real concern for their safety and paid only perfunctory attention to their chatter. If the need arose, a mental summons would bring them to his side.

They were worthy beasts, and badly in need of exercise. They had long been patient while Hult sat with the silent forms of past elders in the dreaming-place of the Bachan, letting the faculties of his nithbrog unfold. Hult had had no time to spare for his beasts then, for he was lost in the new inner life. For a time, when the first weakness and death-feeling had passed and his outer senses grew hyperacute, he had been in great pain and turmoil as his mind and body were bombarded by signals from an external reality that seemed suddenly to have doubled and redoubled in extent and intensity. But he had learned to harness the new senses and mental powers that developed in the last great phase of Onhla life. Nithbrog came to few, and now it had come to Hult. He felt the potent glory of his new state, but wondered still why he had received the boon. There was much still to learn.

A twinge of hunger came to him from the koomiok, resolving into a plea that they be permitted to broach the food cache they had sensed ahead of them. Hult allowed it, and at once the exultant anticipation of meat taste, crunching bones between the broad jaws, and a full belly flowed from

their simple minds. Now, in nithbrog, he understood his
beasts differently and far more clearly than he ever had before. There was no complexity in them; their drives were
basic and unmasked. Appetite, always; sudden flarings of
lust and anger; a great awe for their Onhla masters and especially for Hult, who had brought their forebears to this
wonderful world from a sparse and scanty wasteland among
the lights overhead. They could not even remotely comprehend the truth of their origin, but a simple tale had passed
from dam and sire on to the first cubs, and then to their
cubs and all who came after. By now it was myth, their own
origin story, and inviolable. Hult had often listened to its
telling, watched the long narrow eyes widen as they turned
to him and saw the one who had brought their race from the
old place. He was their god, the deliverer of the koomiok,
first and greatest of his tribe.

And now he had passed from the age of progenitor to become an ancient, huge in size, immensely powerful, and
gifted with senses unsuspected in his earlier phases. For the
first time, he was aware of his individuality. He was Hult, he
was unique and alone. His name had a meaning, and he had
a life apart from his tribe. And with the thrill of identity, he
felt its loneliness. But Treborra would soon reach her turning point; if she survived and changed, they would be together as never before. It would be their best time, the cul-
mination of pairing; total unity of being.

Hult could understand others to their depths now, but it
was difficult for one in nithbrog to communicate except with
those in the same life-phase. The wisdom moved within, and
only those who shared the inward senses could share their
fruits. To speak to others was like speaking to cubs, or to
those who knew only bits and fragments of Onhla speech.
They could not understand.

But two in nithbrog were closer than any others could
ever be. Even in the moments when they lay locked together on their bed of soft pelts, creating from their union

the life of a new tribe, they could not experience the total intimacy of mind touching mind, sharing impressions of outside and reflections from within in a full new way, with deep comprehension. That was possible only in nithbrog, and for Hult and Treborra, it had not yet come. Hult, in his full strength, fast approaching the peak of his mental powers, was alone of his kind and might be so forever.

He was aware of his isolation, but he did not bemoan his fate. Onhla did not do such things. They bore what befell. To live was to endure: that was the first wisdom. And they had endured much.

Hult thought of their firstborn, who had died without a whimper, even though the tulk had gored him horribly. At the time, it seemed senseless.

Hult relived the moment with exact clarity. It was on the first hunt of that dark. The tulk were moving in great numbers and food was abundant. They need not have pursued that last fine specimen, with his mask of bristling horns and his clublike tail. But they had run him down, four of the young and their pack of koomiok. The great beast had staggered the bold young hunter with a blow of his tail and struck at once with his horns.

But despite this death, and the deaths of others, the tribe lived still. The oldest were already in their haldrim, and a new generation were gaining strength and skill. Endurance was all.

Hult was learning to see death in a new way. Like all things, it was changed for him forever. When he sat among the frozen remains of those past generations, absorbing their wisdom and their long experience, the pain had at times been so great as to tear at his sanity. Every nerve and every sense seemed flayed to agonizing sensitivity. But he endured, and at last, in a rapturous instant, had come enlightenment.

Barriers had fallen within him, walls crumbled, gates flung wide. Senses had dissolved and commingled to nourish and augment one another. All that had gone before, Hult now comprehended in a new way, and he saw the wonder and the necessity of what was to come. There was no death for an Onhla, there was a translation to a new level of racial communion. The peace of the last long dreaming, when the stillness came and all things were clear, flickered in his mind like the skyblaze on the horizon, a tantalizing foretaste of the final wisdom. All without became realer, revealed itself more fully, and his new inner senses plumbed the deepest truths. Pain was forgotten in the flood of ecstatic awakening.

But as yet he could share it with no one. The new wisdom would be joined to the knotted annals of the tribe, but none would fully understand until they came to nithbrog.

Hult trudged on at a steady pace, a moving monolith amid the leveling wind and terrible cold. To him, the blast was a gentle breeze and the bitter temperature was balmy. He could endure far worse now. He seemed a creature made of elemental frost: his skin was a pale blue, his long hair and the fur that grew thick over his shoulders and on his upper limbs was white, and his towering body was wrapped in a single garment of smoke-gray gorwol fur. He sensed no discomfort, only a growing eagerness to rejoin the tribe. He longed to read the knots of the past and unlock their mysteries with his new powers.

Something plucked at his mind.

It was faint and far away, and it came and passed in an instant, but something had been there . . . a summons . . . a warning. He ranged the koomiok and found them motionless ahead. Touching their minds, he received only emanations of satisfaction. They were still now, sated with meat. Narik, the male, was feeling the first faint stirrings of desire for the female, Dengar, but she was not yet ready, and she snapped at his advances. Hult commanded them to restore the food cache and wait by it until he arrived. All their other sensations vanished in a rush of compliance. He damped them out and went on, musing over the things he had experienced among the silent forms of the Bachan dreamers.

Again, more sharply, something stung his attention. He stopped in his tracks. The koomiok, too, seemed to have sensed something, but so faintly that it was undecipherable. They felt uneasy, and did not know why. Hult threw his mind open to everything around him. There was only the silence of Starside, the pressure of the wind, the dull half-life of the things that lived deep below, and the uneasy sensations of the koomiok. He focused his consciousness tightly and sent it to the farthest limit his senses could reach. Something was there. His mind clutched, but the thing slipped away; he was not yet full master of his new powers. He cast forth again, and felt . . . pain. A great amazement, sudden pain, confusion . . . then nothing.

An Onhla was in grave danger.

Hult hurried to the food cache, reopened it, and removed a haunch of tulk. The koomiok, their bellies full, looked on dully as he slashed strips from the frozen meat and hung them by his side, to keep. A long journey lay ahead, and they were going by the hard direct way, where no food awaited. Hult resealed the cache, and tearing off a piece of meat with his teeth, moved on, toward the summons.

They traveled steadily over the ice fields, moving more swiftly than any other creature could hope to move in Starside. They climbed the hills and crossed the long plateau, then descended to the frozen plain, and all the time no signal came. Hult felt doubt; perhaps his new senses were deceiving him with uncomprehended powers. He lightly scanned the koomioks' memories and was assured. They, too, had heard the signal.

He pressed on, up the last rise, and from the last ridge he saw the Onhla encampment. For an instant he stood immobilized by the sight before him, then he plunged headlong down the slope.

Bodies lay everywhere, Onhla and koomiok alike, torn

and mangled and disfigured. The beasts had been hastily skinned, and their carcasses resembled naked humanoid bodies grotesquely elongated and flattened. The Onhla had been stripped of their outer garments and lay in unnatural postures amid curling tessellations of frozen blood. Their bodies had been hacked and rent by powerful weapons. No life remained here.

Hult moved among the dead, seeking Treborra. He found her at the center of a small ring of bodies. Something had blown away most of her head, and one thigh was mangled. She lay on her back, twisted with her final agonies. Icicles of blood rose from her torn face.

Beside her lay a human from Norion, his neck broken. Another lay nearby, his head crushed. This one, Hult did not recognize at once. His garments were like the others', but they bore strange markings. He was not of Hraggellon.

Hult inspected the camp and found other humans, but no more of the unfamiliar ones. The destruction was complete. All the adults were dead, and most of the young. The rest were missing. Every gorwol pelt was gone; the shelters were leveled and all the goods were smashed, the fragments scattered. The knotted annals of the tribe lay in pieces, hacked into finger-sized bits of leather.

The past of the tribe was destroyed. If the missing young were dead, then the Onhla were ended for all time. Hult threw back his head and raised his massive fists to the stars and gave a cry of pain.

He stood among the ruin and felt himself sink into utter despair and a great confusion. His new powers could not help. A thing like this had never happened on Hraggellon, and he could not fathom the reason for it. All things had a reason, but what could explain this? He knew that the humans of Norion did such things to one another in their contests for power, but they had never attacked Onhla before. Why now? Why such ferocity? And who was the stranger?

It took time for his mind to restore itself after the awful

shock, and then he began to learn. He probed deeply into the tangled skein of consciousness that still lay like an invisible mist over the scene. He picked and sorted the strands and pieced together images. First, surprise at the sight of mounted humans so deep in Starside, and the sudden fear of the unfamiliar. Then Treborra's reassurance, and the welcome to the newcomers. There followed mingling, and speech, and the humans penetrated to every part of the camp. Then the shock and horror, bursts of pain, and a sensation that bit into his mind and drew forth an agonized groan. Hatred, like a caustic dashed on raw flesh, burning and eating ever deeper.

Hult had never experienced such a thing before. Onhla did not harbor such feelings toward other living beings. Hatred was a defiance of the order of things. But these attackers, whoever they were, had come filled with hatred, like vessels of poison.

Hult took up the strange body and studied it closely. The odd black garment it wore came off to reveal a black uniform within, and his memory, now nearly perfect, at once brought back the long ago voyage to Insgar. The humans on the white ship had worn such garments; not the traders but the others, the ones with the weapons at their sides. Such weapons would wreak carnage like the scene around him.

He probed the dead mind, but it was opaque; perhaps his new powers did not extend to something so alien, or perhaps the manner of the creature's death had disrupted all traces of consciousness and deprived him of the long dreaming. Whatever the cause, his mind revealed nothing.

Hult had to know. The massacre had occurred only a short time ago, and the marauders could not be far. He could track them by his ordinary senses, with the assistance of his beasts, but that way was slow, and even for him, open to error. He could afford no error now.

Again, he opened his mind to all sensation. He listened long, but nothing came. He narrowed to a tightly focused beam of consciousness and sent it out like a light probing the darkness. Deep into Starside he cast his mind, and found nothing. He poured all his will into the probe, and as he turned toward Brightside, he felt a flicker of response.

The mind that he touched was a very young mind and it was helpless with fear, unaware of his outreaching consciousness. Fear . . . and struggle. Pain, but not the pain of injury . . . the pain of restraint, that was it. Other young minds opened to him as he homed in more surely. Young Onhla, prisoners of the raiders, being led off to Starside. Captives . . . but alive. The tribe was not dead, and if they could be rescued, the Onhla might be reborn yet once more.

One duty remained. Hult gathered the torn and mangled remains of his tribe and seated them in a row, facing Starside. At the midpoint of the line of corpses, well ahead of them, he kindled a great dreamfire from all the debris of the camp.

As the flame sank, Hult turned away. He signaled to Narik and Dengar. Cautiously, slinking low, they came to his side. They were confused and fearful, and he laid his hands on their broad skulls to comfort them. The beasts grew calm and received his orders. At the command, they burst forward in the direction of Brightside, and Hult followed in their tracks.

The raiders were many, and Hult was alone. He was stronger than their strongest, but he was not invulnerable. They were armed with weapons capable of terrible destruction, and he bore only his wrist blades. But he carried within him the power of nithbrog. It grew stronger with each breath he took, and as the power increased, so did his understanding and mastery of it. The wisdom of the dreamers was his armor and his strength.

. . . spectacular auroral displays commonly called *skyblaze*, visible when the shadowline is at its deepest incursion at midlight . . . said to have saved the lives of one hunting party by serving as a beacon toward Brightside.

Unusual light and visual effects combine with weather to make Starside travel extremely hazardous. Sudden envelopment of absolute darkness and . . . interference with instruments . . . particularly dangerous. [Analogues: Old Earth *whiteout* and *fata morgana;* seasonal blindstorms on Loki.] Terms used by natives, such as *Belt of Deception, Starburn,* and *Eye-bite,* tend to demoralize and undermine confidence, and we have banned their use.

Despite known and postulated difficulties, we believe that Sternverein cold-climate suits type D-6, properly used, will enable our forces to operate securely and effectively in the coldest regions of Hraggellon [cf. ordnance report, Nemesis Run B641 to Hingwoll, a/C Ryne].

B-V Jarmal, Tech I

Tenth Hraggellon

XI.

THE FEAR WITHIN

A cataract of icy wind poured from the plateau, swept across the plain, and buffeted the long line of beasts and men moving slowly into Starside. The shaggy, heavy-bodied haxopods plodded forward at a steady pace, but even they were staggered now and again by a sudden blast of more than the usual force. Twice the caravan's progress halted while the men reloaded sledges that had been toppled by a sudden gust and had their contents strewn across the frozen surface.

Clell Basedow cursed for the thousandth time this world, its weather, and all its inhabitants, and turned the controls of his cold-climate suit a notch higher. The desolation was beyond anything he had ever imagined. Eternal darkness, with nothing but stars overhead and the wild skyblaze dancing on the Brightside horizon to show the way; cold, and an icy relentless wind, and flat frozen ground; no sound but the roaring of that wind and one's own labored breath . . . awful.

By the uncertain light of his bobbing head lamp, he studied the young Onhla, trussed in pairs and each pair carried on a haxopod. They were silent and sullen, unable to communicate with one another and unwilling to speak to others. Terrified, he assumed, having witnessed the slaughter of their tribe and not knowing what awaited them. They ought to be grateful, and not merely for the sparing of their lives. Clell Basedow was doing these hateful creatures a service, taking them from that desolation and forcing upon them an opportunity to live a useful life in the service of the Sternverein. It grated on him to think of a single Onhla being spared, but even in his revenge, Clell was practical. These things would be Onhla in appearance and physical make-up only. The name would be eradicated. Their race was extinct forever, its history destroyed utterly, its home obliterated. Nothing of the Onhla remained but these dozen cubs, scarcely more than baby animals. And they would be raised by Clell's own trainers in Norion, to do his bidding. They would hunt for him, serve him . . . perhaps one day they would be made his bodyguards. The irony gratified him, and he smiled a rare smile.

"Something pleases you?" Orm asked, at his side.

"Yes," Clell said, startled. He had not noticed the other's approach. "Yes, everything pleases me so far. Except this climate."

"Worse than you imagined, isn't it? Now you know why we of Norion leave this waste to fugitives and beasts."

"Our suits will protect us," Clell said.

"So you say. The communicators have ceased to operate, and we're scarcely past the shadowline. What goes wrong next?"

"There's nothing wrong with the communicators, it's all the outside interference. Those blasted lights on the horizon, or perhaps mineral concentrations in the ground. The suits won't fail us."

"They've worked so far," Orm admitted, "but the worst is before us. We must go well into Starside to cut off the Remembrancers' escape. They'll never expect us to attack from ahead."

Clell gestured toward the young Onhla. "What of these creatures? Will they survive such cold?"

"This is their home. They've dwelt here since Norion was only a collection of clay huts on the riverbank, and long before that. They'll survive."

Clell nodded, and said nothing in reply. They rode on in silence for a time, intent on keeping their staggering mounts on the trail against the battering of the wind. When it died down, Orm spoke.

"That was good sport, raiding the Onhla. Better than riding down a lot of squealing Remembrancers. We lost a few men, but we can spare them. By Wuran, they put up a fight!"

"They killed one of my men."

"You're lucky they didn't get more. Even those cubs are vicious little creatures. What will you do with them?"

"Train them. One day they'll hunt at my bidding."

Orm bared his teeth in a ferocious grin. "They may hunt you instead. Onhla have long memories."

"When I'm finished training them, they'll remember only what I permit them to remember."

Orm studied him for a moment, and said, "You hate the Onhla very much. Was it an Onhla that broke your back?"

"I hate Onhla no more and no less than you hate Remembrancers. I wanted the cubs and could not get them otherwise," Clell replied, choosing to reveal nothing more to this barbarian.

Orm's anger flared at once. "The Onhla present no danger to you, as the Remembrancers do to me. You raided them for gain, and the promise of more gain, and my forces joined you for the sport of the hunt. Make no comparisons where none fits. The Remembrancers keep alive the times before the first Orm came to rule in Norion. They preserve old ways, and the old ways are not my ways. They must be forgotten. While Remembrancers live, the old ways live, too, and threaten the welfare of Norion."

"True, Benefactor," Clell said in a placating voice. "It's wisdom that moves you to eliminate them. Every wise ruler sees the necessity of destroying all traces of what has been done before. It serves to pacify his subjects."

Orm relaxed a bit. "This was the custom of Old Earth. You spoke of it yourself. And Vessius of the Three Worlds did likewise."

"True, Benefactor. You do as you must."

"The Remembrancers are a danger. They must be removed," Orm said firmly.

Clell did not reply. He was well pleased with himself. Orm was the perfect puppet. He snatched up every hint, accepted every insinuation, acted on every urging. With the proper handling, he would be no trouble at all to the Sternverein, and within his limitations, fairly useful.

If only his world were not such a bleak and bitter place, Clell reflected. One great chunk of it buried in eternal cold and darkness, another portion forever baking under a sun that never set, seas that raged and churned so furiously that no boat could navigate them, and only a narrow strip of land where humans could live at all as humans should, with a day and a night and seasons. Even there, the cold was too cold, the heat too hot for normal existence. Dark and light seemed interminable in Norion.

And yet life clung to this world, and endured. Not only in Norion, but in the wastes of shadowlands, right to the rim of Starside; even beyond, life went on, humans and beasts and even plants. Clell had seen them stir to life before his eyes, at the first touch of the advancing light. He had marveled at his first sight of those great gaping trumpets of blackness drinking in the far faint beams of early brighttime, and at the blazing beauty of the firebloom, flickering red and gold against the bleakness surrounding it. Even the hungry tendrils of the heat-thief, crawling to the warmth of a passing body, and the clutching spines of never-go-free, repellent as their touch might be, were living and fighting to live on.

But the Onhla would live no more. They were extinct even now, for these trussed-up cubs were not the last of the Onhla, they were the first of a nameless, deracinated breed of servants. The Onhla were gone forever from this world, and the Remembrancers would soon join them in oblivion.

Orm left Clell's side and rode ahead. He was gone for some time, and then the caravan came to a disorderly halt, clustering in little knots of snorting beasts and silent men. Head lamp beams flashed in all directions. Clell rode forward to where Orm and the scouts and leader were gathered and joined their conference.

With Orm's shouts and accusations, the angry protestations of the lead rider, and the fragmented, interrupted reports of the scouts mixed in his ears, and the ears closely muffled against the cold, it took a few moments for Clell to learn the difficulty. A wide crevasse lay diagonally across their path, and opinion was divided as to whether the expedition should ride right, toward Brightside, or left, and deeper into Starside than they had planned. To ride toward Brightside was to backtrack; it might lose them the advantage of surprise; but it would be safer. The cold was growing steadily more bitter, and to ride much further into Starside was to risk overexposure.

The men of Norion settled differences chiefly by outshouting the opposition. With the suit radios out of commission, Clell had no choice but to add his voice to the clamor.

He spoke for the turn to Brightside. His own objective had been attained, and he had no wish to brave further cold. He saw the opportunity of proceeding directly back to Norion with his trophies and leaving the others to ride on after the Remembrancers.

The babble raged for some time, until Clell and the Brightside faction seemed to have carried the day. And then, in the midst of the final wrangling, a chill ran through Clell Basedow that had nothing to do with the wind and the cold of Starside. An icy hand passed lightly over his consciousness and then moved on, and he was left with an overwhelming horror at the thought of turning toward the light. Something unknown and awful awaited him there, and he could not face it.

The uproar ceased abruptly. In the sudden quiet Clell looked around, and when he saw the faces of the men of Norion, he knew that they had felt it, too.

"We go to Starside," Orm commanded, and rode on ahead.

The men obeyed eagerly, without a word of dissent, and the long caravan became an orderly line once more and moved on. Clell took his place at the head of the supply sledges, behind the last of the captive Onhla, and before long Orm fell in beside him. The silence stretched out until it was too uncomfortable to endure, and Clell broke it.

"Did you feel it, too?" he asked.

"Feel what?" Orm said truculently. "I felt only the cold."

"Something inside . . . fear . . . a foreboding."

Orm was silent for a time; then, in a lower voice, he said, "Yes, I felt it. Something is waiting out there to destroy us if we turn to Brightside."

"What is it? How could we all feel it?"

Orm half-mumbled, half-growled an unintelligible reply and jerked his mount aside, leaving Clell's question unanswered. Clell sank into deep thought, uneasy at this sudden touch of irrational fear. The line of beasts and men moved on, toward the Great Rift, deeper into the dark cold of Starside.

Far away, Hult paused and opened his consciousness to the feelings of the marauders. He had touched them cautiously, seeking some hint of their motives and their plans, but their alien minds were locked tight against him. He had felt them shrink from his presence, and withdrawn himself at once, after no more than a momentary experience of turbulent emotion. Now he ranged them moving into Starside, and wondered, as he had wondered when he ranged them turning in that direction. These were humans and otherworlders, who had always shunned Starside. Could they all be mad? There was a mystery here.

Hult could not penetrate the murky veil of alien will, nor could he empathize with the jangled emotions of those breeds. They were too different. He could only reach out and offer contact. Admitted to a concordant mind, he could link consciousness with the other in a silent conversation of merging intuitions; rejected, he instinctively drew back and left the other inviolate.

He stood long, pondering, and then set off in pursuit, the koomiok rippling over the ground at his side. Whatever drove the humans, he had to follow. He did not yet know how he would accomplish it, but his duty was clear. The young had to be rescued; the marauders had to be stopped; the danger had to be removed.

Clell Basedow passed from deep brooding into a half-doze, and the awareness of a rider at his side brought him awake with a start. He blinked at the young over-lieutenant, who looked back at him impassively without a trace of fear. There would be no reactions from him, Clell realized, except aggression and self-preservation.

Like all the troopers, Over-lieutenant Tassur had under-gone the Nolo treatment. Basedow, exempt because of his rank, suspected and disapproved of Nolo, though he admit-ted the disciplinary necessity. He considered the treatment as dulling to the mind as to the feelings, and spoke with the troopers as little as possible. They rode before and behind, in guard positions, with Orm's own men. Clell sensed a ri-valry between the two forces, but knew that there would be no breach of Sternverein discipline. And if the dog-faced troops from Norion forgot themselves, he was certain that his security troopers would make short work of them. No worry there.

"What's the trouble, Over-lieutenant?" he asked curtly.

"Has there been a change of plan, sir?"

"There has not. We're still going to hit the Remembrancers from ahead."

"We're turning into Starside, sir. The original plan was—"

"There's a crevasse ahead, Tassur. It's too deep to cross. We can go to the left or the right, and we decided to go left. We'll resume march once we're over."

"Yes, sir. Thank you, sir."

Clell returned his salute, and the over-lieutenant turned his mount and rode to the rear of the long column. Did he feel that touch of dread? Clell wondered. Does the Nolo make them immune to fear as well as love and pity? Almost worth trying, if it does. That clutching horror . . . I don't want that again.

They made steady progress, and stopped for a long encampment when the rising wind slowed them to a crawl. Shelters were erected only after a hard struggle, but a hearty meal, eaten within those flimsy walls, raised everyone's spirits. The fireblocks burned bright with a reassuring steady glow that defied the powers of wind, cold, and darkness. When Clell awoke, he learned that the scouts had found a safe crossing, and they could expect to be over the crevasse and heading toward Brightside before the next encampment. He was much relieved by this news. He trusted the cold-climate suits and the fireblocks, and he knew their supplies were ample, but this place unnerved him. They were no more than four long marches into Starside, but that was far enough. Starside was no place for humans, and he longed to leave it behind him.

They reached the crossing just at the time of the midmeal and stopped on the far side to eat and to rest briefly. Then, feeling renewed physically and mentally, they turned their faces toward Brightside.

Hult came to the crevasse and paused. He knew a clear trail on the opposite side, and a crossing would not be difficult, but he was not certain what the humans intended. If they wished only to cross the crevasse, they could have done so more easily by turning toward Brightside at the outset. For a time, until they rested, he followed their trail. He ranged others, a small party, riding ahead until they came to a place where mounts could cross. It was clear, then, that they meant only to make their way to the other side, and then they would return. This was odd behavior, even for humans and otherworlders.

He touched the cubs' minds, one by one, without revealing himself. They were less unsettled now, and he felt their anticipation, like a certain knowledge that he would deliver them. He sent assurance flowing through them until they were calm. Then he eased himself down into the crevasse, made his slow way up the opposite face, and settled down to await the caravan.

The glow on the horizon was far and faint, but unmistakable. Brightside lay before them, and somewhere along their way was the ragtag caravan of Remembrancers. If they headed directly toward the coastal trail, they would be certain to cut off the fugitives. A short skirmish, and then it was full speed back to Norion, the mission a total success.

Clell became aware of warmth, and checked his suit indicator. He was surprised to note that all unthinking, he had turned it to intensity ten, two notches from maximum. He reduced it at once. Only a few marches into Starside, and he had had to run it that high . . . the thought troubled him. He wore the Sternverein's most efficient cold-climate gear. If Starside grew colder as one penetrated more deeply, then even the suits would not take them far. He marveled anew at the hostility of this world. At least the worst was behind them, and they would be back in Norion before long. The city was no paradise. It was a glorified burrow, suited to its nasty-smelling denizens; but it was sheltered and warm. A man could attempt a life there.

During the mid-meal rest, scouts returned with news of the terrain. Other crevasses had been located, but these would prove no obstacle; they required only a slight turn to Brightside, not a long, cold detour like the one just completed.

Clell finished his rations and stretched his bare hands out to the blazing fireblock. It was impossible to eat with those heavy gloves on, and yet one's fingers grew numb in moments once they were exposed. He saw Orm approaching, mounted, with three of his guards, and stood to greet him.

Suddenly a current of terror ran through him, so violent and overwhelming in its intensity that he cried aloud, staggered, and gasped for breath. His stomach revolted at the shock. He fell to his knees, gagging and coughing brokenly, choking and whimpering like a terrified animal in sick fear and helplessness. As he struggled to his feet he heard all around him the cries of panic wrung from the others. Orm and his guards were already riding off at top speed. Beasts were plunging and rearing nearby, threatening to break loose. Clell raced to them and flung himself on one, jerking the reins free. The haxopod, catching his fear, wheeled and set off at a run into Starside on the track of Orm.

Shouts rose behind Clell Basedow, but he ignored them. Nothing mattered but flight. He had to get away from that blast of awful terror. No man could face the cause of that and survive whole and sane. He rode on, urging the beast with kicks and cries.

Twice again in that nightmarish flight the fear penetrated him like a toxin suffusing his bloodstream. His mind blanked out, and he rode on oblivious, tossed and bruised by the haxopod's bounding stride, his hands deep in the beast's coat, clinging for his life.

They had gone some distance before his head cleared and he realized that he could not feel his hands. All sensation was gone. When he pulled them loose from the shaggy coat of the haxopod, he saw that his fingers were unnaturally white; and they were completely numb. Where patches of flesh had been torn off, there was no bleeding.

The exhausted haxopod had slowed its pace by this time. Even so, its gait was uneven. Clumsily, with his dead fingers, atop a pitching mount, Clell drew the gloves from his thigh pocket and worked his hands into them, pulling them into place with his teeth. Soon his hands would begin to pain him, he knew, but that could be borne. Anything could be endured that brought him away from the source of that awful fear.

He rode on, following the track of Orm's little party, and it came to him with sudden clarity that they were all going to die. They could not return to Brightside, and Starside meant inevitable cold death. The end was drawing near for all of them, and Clell thought of it with an unexpected sense of resignation, almost of welcome.

Once again the humans had turned and fled into Starside, and their flight was the deed of madmen. Hult searched inwardly, but his experience, and the lore of the Onhla, offered no helpful parallel. These outsiders acted in their own unreasoning ways, and the answers lay with them. Hult reached out, and each mind he touched threw off waves of feeling he could not interpret, products of an alien mental pattern impenetrable even to Onhla senses. Something was assaulting these minds from within and dividing them against themselves. They came from Brightside and longed to return to Brightside—the typical Brightsider's yearning for warmth and enclosure and stillness saturated their thoughts—and yet they fled from Brightside as if it held all the horrors of the universe. There was something of madness in this.

He sought an explanation, and at length it occurred to him that he himself might be causing the fear. But this seemed most unlikely. An Onhla could bring a stillness upon his quarry, making death painless, but that was done only to beasts. These creatures were humans, and Hult did not believe that he could so affect them. He had not attempted to force communication with the marauders, or to blend minds as he would with Onhla. He had merely tapped the surface of their consciousness; peered, as it were, through a pinhole into the closed confines behind the barrier of alienness and identity and outward behavior. Surely his muted momentary presence in their minds could not cause such irrational behavior. It was far more likely that whatever incomprehensible urge had led them to massacre his tribe and carry off the young had also driven them into the fatal cold of Starside. Perhaps it was memur, or a penitential self-destruction such as was practiced by false Remembrancers, or a mass urge to commence the long dreaming. He could not decide, and so he set the problem aside. Other matters were more pressing.

In their headlong flight, the raiders had abandoned their prisoners, and the young Onhla had taken advantage of their opportunity. They could communicate only in the most rudimentary fashion with the haxopods, but the beasts accepted their direction. When the panic of the humans began to infect the haxopods, some who bore the Onhla were able to resist. They carried the prisoners off, far from their captors, scattering in all directions. But many of the Onhla had calmed the beasts, freed themselves, and begun to seek their companions.

Hult sent his presence forth to all his tribe. Their minds opened to him, and all became one mind with his, and he felt the relief and gratitude and sense of deliverance that welled up in them. He touched each one, from tiny Sholot to big, gruff Roilan, assuring, reaffirming their liberation, and ordering them to assemble at the raiders' abandoned campsite.

He withdrew from their minds then, and ranged them one by one. The farthest were already hurrying back, gathering in little clusters to return together.

But some had never left the campsite, and now he turned to these, whose minds had not responded to his touch. He probed more deeply, and found only emptiness. They had gone too early into the long dreaming, and left nothing behind. One lay crushed beneath haxopods who had stumbled in their panic. Another had been taken over the rim of the crevasse by terrified beasts; one had died inexplicably. And yet the others lived; this was good that helped soften the loss.

He set off for the campsite to meet the returning young. Upon arriving at the scene of disarray, he cast about him once more for a sign of the raiders. In their madness, they were capable of anything, and might even now be returning.

They were not. He ranged none close by, but what he found surprised him. A small, tight caravan, men and beasts and supply sledges, was moving in an orderly manner along the trail the frenzied fugitives had taken. They had escaped Hult's notice before, in his preoccupation with the fugitives and the Onhla, but now he investigated. He reached out to probe them and found them opaque to his senses. The minds of the others had boiled with the indecipherable emotions of humans; these minds, though human, were like tablets of ice. Nothing moved in them. And yet they followed the others, were part of the others, and even now were on their way to join the mad fugitives.

The ways of humans were unfathomable. Whether they be of Norion, or otherworlders, men were beyond the ken of even the ancient Onhla wisdom, Hult judged. He, who had spent more time among men than any Onhla of this world, realized anew how little he had learned of them.

But these were thoughts for another time. Now was the time to see to the needs of his tribe.

The wind had fallen and the way was clear. Tassur and his force of troopers rode at a steady gait along the track left by Clell Basedow. It was a meandering, confused trail, crossing and recrossing an earlier track, but they followed it diligently. Basedow was Mission Primary; their first duty was to protect him. As the trail became more regular, Tassur sent scouts out well ahead of the sledges. The beasts had to be spared as much as possible; if they were lost, no one would return to Brightside.

Even with all the beasts, it would be hard going and short

rations for this expedition from now on, with only two sledges of supplies left, and those not half-full. The others had been scattered in all directions when that madness struck the camp for the second time. It had affected them all much more strongly than before; the first time, in fact, Tassur had almost missed the sudden blankness of Basedow's eyes, the paling of his face. But not when it struck again.

Tassur wondered, but formed no hypotheses. He was no predicator, but a trooper. Whatever the others had felt, he and his troopers had been untouched. Perhaps it was the Nolo treatment that made them immune; he preferred to credit courage and discipline, but could not be certain. Little as he regarded Orm's overfed guardsmen, it pained him to see trained warriors fleeing in panic from an unseen menace, weapons dangling unused at their sides. There was shame in that, and no Sternverein trooper could do it.

And it was an unseen menace, something beyond the senses, he was certain of that much. Here in this place of starlight and skyblaze there were strange sights to set a man to questioning his senses. Cliffs and mountains rose where none existed, and yet the eye saw them. Eerie sounds, too, from a wind that raced over half a world unimpeded until it made the ground sing and moan in its passage. But the fear was none of these.

The track was straight now, and the little caravan drew together. Soon a distant figure came into view. Tassur tried his suit communicator once again. It was silent, as it had been since they passed into Starside. But the figure caught sight of their lights, halted, and waved stiffly before moving on at a slower pace. They closed on him rapidly.

Tassur saluted, and Clell returned the salute with a clumsy gesture and listened calmly to the report. "The troopers are all present and accounted for, sir. We've salvaged two sledges, partially loaded. Enough to get us back safely, if we return directly," the Over-lieutenant said.

"Back? To face that?" Clell asked.

"To face what, sir? I saw the panic, and I tried to find out why all the others ran, but it was impossible. One of Orm's men tried to cut me down when I blocked his way."

"You felt nothing, Tassur? Nothing at all? No sudden fear?"

"None of the troopers felt anything, sir."

"Then bless the man who invented the Nolo treatment, Over-lieutenant," Clell said, and his voice was haunted. "It's spared you a horror beyond description."

"Sir, if there's a threat, we're ready to face it. That's our duty. Whatever it is, it can't stand up to a Sternverein attack team. We'll keep a double guard all the way back."

"Tassur, there's no power in the universe that can make me face that fear again. Besides, we can't go back without Orm's men to lead us."

"We need only head for the Brightside horizon, sir."

Clell was adamant. "Never, Over-lieutenant. If you had felt what I felt, you'd have no questions."

"If we go further into Starside we may all die there, sir," Tassur said calmly.

"I'll face anything, as long as . . . We can't return without Orm, at any rate," Clell said. "Norion is his domain, we left it together, and we must return together, even if we carry only his frozen corpse. The Sternverein does not want to lose this planet."

"No, sir."

"Very well. We will camp here for one full march, then set out on Orm's trail. He's spoken of alternate return routes, and once we're together again we'll plan our way back. What of the prisoners, Tassur? Did you bring them, too?"

"Their beasts panicked and took them off, sir. My first concern was for the supplies. We lost two full sledge loads into the crevasse. A pair of prisoners went over, too."

Clell said softly, "So much for the Onhla. Over-lieutenant," he ordered sharply, "detail a man to prepare my shelter and food. My hands are frozen, and I can't use them. I'll need help."

"At once, sir. If I may suggest, sir, you'd be wise to stay here and let us go ahead to seek Orm. The Mission Primary should take no risks."

"It's a necessary risk, Over-lieutenant. Orm will deal only with the Mission Primary. It's my duty to go," Basedow said. This was true, but it was not his real reason. He wanted to move as far as he could, even into Starside, from that paralyzing menace that had shaken his mind and rendered him insensible with fear. The flight might cost him his life; it would almost certainly cost him his hands; but he could not turn and face the horror.

The Berkenson treatment . . . not only eliminates the sexual drive in mature males and females of all humanoid races ranking 0.94 and above on the Racial Cognate Scale, it also . . . induces a continuous and predictable decline in over-all emotional responsiveness. *Desirable emotions such as aggressiveness can nevertheless be selectively stimulated without difficulty* [see Appendix M and Keitges' tables].

The treatment is permanent until chemically reversed, and those subjected to repeated treatments show no physiological or psychological ill effects [see Appendix J]. On the contrary, they appear stronger in body, clearer in mind, and *less subject to the emotional disturbances* found among deep-space veterans in later life. . . .

Therefore, considering the advantage offered by the Berkenson treatment in enabling the Sternverein to maintain discipline and morale at the necessary level on extended space missions . . . this committee *unanimously recommends immediate adoption of the treatment on a trial basis.*

Report on Project NOLO

Sternverein Training Command, Occuch

CONFIDENTIAL

XII.

THE BECLOUDING

At the end of the third march the Sternverein party came upon Orm and two of his guardsmen huddled around a fireblock. They saw the glow from far off, but their beasts were weary and could not be hurried, and they were a long time in reaching them.

The men of Norion had taken shelter in a niche at the foot of a low ice cliff. The wind, rising now, howled over and around them. The fireblock flame whipped and flickered in the churning drafts. No one greeted Clell Basedow as he stumbled into their encampment and sank to his knees before the flame.

At length Orm said, "What do you bring?"

Clell looked at him uncomprehending, and Orm cried, "What food do you carry on those sledges? What fireblocks? Do you bring shelters?"

"Some food, some fireblocks. Not much. The supplies were scattered. My troopers salvaged all they could," Clell said wearily.

Orm gestured to his guardsmen. "Go, help them unload and set up shelters."

As the guardsmen trudged off, hunched against the wind, Clell said, "Whatever we bring, it will have to last until we find some other way to Brightside. I won't go back where that horror might touch me again."

"Nor will I. We'll continue into Starside until we can descend into the Great Rift. Once we're inside we'll be sheltered, and we can get food through the ice. We'll work our way to Brightside in the Rift, then return to Norion along the coastal trail and the caravan route," Orm said.

"Have we any chance of making it?"

Orm did not answer at once. Finally he said in a lower

voice, "Not all of us. With your supplies, we may have enough to make it to the Rift, if we cut our rations to minimum survival level. Even then, we're going to lose men."

"So we're finished, either way."

"We are not finished until all are dead," Orm said flatly.

Clell sighed and shook his head. "If we go further into Starside, to the Rift, some of us will die. I believe that. If we turn back . . . we can't turn back . . . that horror, whatever it is . . . I can't face it again. We're lost. Can't you see that?"

"If you think so, stay here. More food for us that way. It's your fault that we're here, anyway," Orm said. Then, as he thought on this, he went on, vehemently. "It was you who led me to hunt down the Remembrancers. I had no hatred for them. Harmless chattering fools, that's all they are, but you tricked me into believing they were a danger."

"You came willingly."

"You used me and my forces. You want the Onhla working for you, taking pelts from Hraggellon, draining our wealth while you fill our city with the trash of other worlds in payment. I've lost men and beasts, and it's your doing, all of it. I'd be in Norion now . . . I'd be . . ." His voice had risen, and he broke off suddenly, panting, inarticulate in his rage. "You've brought us to this!" he said, rising and standing menacingly over Basedow.

The envoy of the Sternverein did not lift his eyes. He only said, "The thing that follows us is not of my doing."

Orm was about to fling an answer back at the otherworlder, but he saw that the men had begun to return and there were many more otherworlders than guardsmen. It was not a time to quarrel.

"What you say is true. This thing menaces all. Let us rest and then make plans," he said, and all accepted his suggestion.

They slept long and upon waking they had a skimpy meal and warmed themselves at a single fireblock. Orm explained his plan in detail, saying nothing about the inevitable losses. Clell seconded this plan, as did Orm's men.

Tassur was unconvinced, and said so bluntly. The others were displeased, but let him speak on, and he offered his own proposal. "I say we must head for Brightside at once. My men will remain on guard all the way. Whatever threatens you will not get past us."

"Has it not touched you, that you can speak so defiantly?" one of the guardsmen demanded.

"I felt nothing, nor did any other trooper. We saw the fear of the others, but it did not reach us, and it will not."

"Easy to speak bravely when you haven't felt that thing . . . groping in your mind," the guardsman said, shuddering.

"That's exactly my point: we haven't felt it, so we can stand up to it and destroy it."

"Nothing can stand up to that . . . that power. It turns the will to water. The mind collapses at its touch," Clell said.

"With respect, sir, I suggest that it may be no more than a sickness. It has not affected all of us, and those—"

"You call me a madman?" Orm cried in fury.

"No, Benefactor, not at all," Tassur said quickly. "I only suggest that some poison, some influence—perhaps the same force that silences our communicators—is causing you suffering and may lcad you to a needless death in Starside."

"Perhaps you otherworlders fear Starside too much," Orm said.

"If we had sufficient rations, I would not hesitate to penetrate deeper into Starside than any man has ever gone before. But I can reckon the amount we need to survive until we reach the Rift, and we have not the third part of that."

"Rations can be reduced. We can make it on minimum rations," Clell pointed out.

"With respect, sir, you speak of starvation rations. I've served on two cold worlds, and I know what a man needs to survive. We do not have it. If we head for the Rift, we will all die before we reach it," Tassur said matter-of-factly.

There was a silence. Orm looked at Clell and the guardsmen. They had known the fear; the troopers could not understand. Tassur observed the leaders and knew that his argument had failed. Reason was a weak opposition to the primal terror the others had felt. He ventured one last way to save his men and the mission.

"One more possibility, if I may speak," he blurted.

"Speak," Orm said.

"For some reason, this thing has had no effect on us, the troopers. Perhaps it's powerless against us. Let us go back, track it down, and kill it. Then all can return safely."

"How will you track it?" Clell asked.

"We'll return to the campsite by the crevasse and start from there. It may be there still."

Clell nodded thoughtfully. This was the most sensible suggestion yet, the only one he found thinkable and with a hope of succeeding. While he pondered, Orm spoke.

"I agree to this. But you must leave at once," said the Benefactor, and Clell then added his agreement.

"We'll take rations for seven marches, and leave the rest here. We should be able to recover more once we're back at the campsite," Tassur said.

He gathered his men and they conferred, then set out, twelve against the cold and a nameless horror. Clell watched until they vanished in the darkness, then turned back to the warmth of the fire. His hands pained him greatly, and he tried to conceal his discomfort from Orm. He felt that the Benefactor of Norion would show little consideration for a disabled man. It would be easy enough to hide his condition except when eating. He decided that he would eat alone, in his shelter.

"Brave men, your troopers," Orm said.

"They are. If it can be found, they'll track it down and destroy it. They fear nothing."

"If it can be found."

Clell looked up. "Of course it can be found. I've never felt such fear before in my life, but that doesn't mean it came from a source we can never find. It only means that there are creatures out here that we don't know, with powers we don't yet understand. I promise you, Benefactor, they'll find it and destroy it, and we'll return safely to Norion."

"They are dead men. It will sweep them away and then come for us, if we remain here."

"It? What is *it*?"

"The maker of the fear. You felt the fear as strongly as I did, and you ran. Do not try to act as brave as your troopers."

Clell looked into the fire and laughed softly, mockingly. "I'm not pretending any courage. I was never so terrified as I was at the crevasse, but I intend to be rational now. We're dead if we move. It won't be any formless horror that kills us, it will be our own stupid panic."

"What do you know?" Orm said contemptuously. "You are not of Hraggellon, you know nothing of its ways and would not trouble to learn them because you think us all beasts and savages. The thing that strikes fear in us might be an ancestral spirit of the Onhla, come to avenge its children. I have heard of such things, and believe they are so. And of frost demons that ride the wind of Starside and suck the warmth from the blood of sleeping men. It might be one of them, driving us to exhaustion and weakness to make us easy prey. And Remembrancers. . . ."

"Remembrancers?" Clell asked in disbelief.

"We have slain Remembrancers, and their elders, their evodes, know ways of summoning things . . . invisible things that move in the darkness."

Clell rose to his feet. He began to laugh. This was absurd. A makeshift king, a barbarian fool who babbled like a child of demons and invisible spirits when the cold was closing in all around them; they were in immediate danger of death from hunger and exposure, and he was reciting a child's litany of night fears. Clell stood unsteadily, for his feet were numb, and said, "Orm . . . a baby who rants of spirits . . . calls himself a ruler. . . . You've come precious little distance from the ways of your tormagon ancestors. Frost demons and ancestral spirits. . . ." He laughed again, louder and more bitingly.

"I am master of Norion, and none laugh at my name!" Orm cried. With a single swift motion, he drew his dagger and drove it up into Clell's chest to the hilt.

Clell's laughter cracked, and he gave a low grunt. He tottered, but remained erect for a moment, looking at Orm with an expression of great surprise on his features. Then he fell forward, directly on top of the fireblock. One of the guardsmen moved toward him, but Orm gestured him away. The stench of burning fabric arose.

"Load the provisions," Orm said to the guard, and to the other, "Get the mounts. We ride at once for the Rift."

Tassur's group moved with disciplined speed and arrived at the campsite at the end of the third long march. They found a wild profusion of tracks and footprints, and one strange pair of tracks that alerted them. They were huge, humanoid, coming alone from Starside and returning to Starside in a direction away from the Rift. But when the creature had left the campsite it was no longer alone. Footprints of young Onhla walked by the intruder's side. Over all were the tracks of a sledge, lightly laden. The traces were faint on the hard ground, but unmistakable to Tassur's experienced eye.

As he weighed these bits of evidence, the last search team returned with news of yet another set of tracks, far off to one side of the rest and steadily parallel to them. "It's a pair of those white beasts we skinned at the Onhla camp," said one trooper.

"Then we've got the young Onhla led off by something

that travels with a pair of their hunting beasts. It must be a mature Onhla that we missed," Tassur said.

"So big? If the footprints are proportionate to size, that thing's enormous—bigger than any Onhla we've ever seen."

"We don't know the limits of Onhla growth, trooper."

"Could it be something else? Some beast nobody's ever seen before?" another trooper asked.

"It could be. Anything's possible on a world like this," Tassur said.

Trooper Graff asked, "Do you think this creature might be what caused all the others to panic?"

Tassur mulled the question over, then shook his head slowly. "I've never heard of anything that could do that to human minds. The Onhla are said to be able to speak to their animals that way, but I've never heard of their doing that to humans."

Casserio, the technical specialist, said, "Maybe it gives off a scent, or some sort of vibrations. Remember the silent singers, on Beta Zotra?"

"Yes. But they affected us even when we were under Nolo. The fear that struck the others didn't touch us at all, and I think the Nolo treatment is what saved us," Tassur replied. "A scent, or vibrations, would have reached us as easily as it got to the others. This thing is implanting emotional reactions; that's why we're untouched."

"Somehow this big beast can reach human minds and create fear. Makes sense," said Casserio. "I've never seen men so terror-stricken in my life."

"Thank the rings for Nolo," murmured Graff.

"Right. So, we're on the trail of this big creature, whatever it is, the young Onhla, and a pair of hunting beasts. As long as the fear can't reach us, we can get him. That track is only about two watches old, and they're drawing a sledge . . . no haxopod tracks, are there?"

"None, Over-lieutenant," several voices answered.

"Then they aren't moving fast. We'll camp here, give the

beasts a good feed and a rest, and set out at top speed in ten hours by chronometer," Tassur said, then snapped out his orders. "Casserio, set up the guard. Two men, two-hour shifts, and they keep moving. If anything approaches, they give the alarm and open fire at once. Kekring, Vuissens, Peyer, start scavenging. We need all the rations and fire-blocks we can get. There's stuff scattered in all directions. Bring it in and load a sledge. Astrur, you and Graff start set-ting the shelters up and get a fire going. Hot food now and when we rise, and for every man going on his guard shift. We've got work ahead."

Sholot and Beleg were the first to succumb. They fell and began to shudder uncontrollably. Hult stopped the little car-avan, sent the others off to a safe distance, and knelt to ex-amine the two cubs.

It was the shaking sickness. Hult knew the symptoms well. Now, in his nithbrog, he was immune, but the younger members of the tribe were not. If it spread to them, this would be the end of the Onhla, after all. He summoned Narik and Dengar, and the two beasts came bounding over the frozen ground to his side, eager for his message.

He laid a hand on each broad skull and placed his thoughts within their minds, gently but ineffaceably. "I must remain here with Sholot and Beleg. Guide the others to the cave on the ledges." He felt their willingness and de-votion pour forth and returned his affection. "A food cache by the long slope, and another by the notch. Do you remem-ber them?" They assured him, and he went on, "Then lead the tribe to safety, and await me in the cave. I will come."

Released from Hult's mental reins, the koomiok sprang forward to where the cubs awaited. Hult blended with the collective mind, ordering obedience to the guides, care of the sledge that bore their rescued gorwol furs, and dutiful obscuring of their tracks. He felt their confusion at this turn of events, and damped the rising uneasiness by projections of all reunited at the great cave complex on the ledges, feasting and hearing the ancient wisdom and planning great hunts together. Their apprehension vanished in the glow of anticipation, and they became anxious to leave. He sent them off with the assurance that he would maintain contact until they were safe at the cave.

As the presence of the others faded, Hult studied the two afflicted cubs, and his spirit darkened. The shaking sickness had long been unknown on Hraggellon, and now a forced contact with humans and otherworlders had resurrected it. Wherever they walked, destruction followed. They seemed fated to destroy all they touched, whether they willed so or not.

Sholot entered the long dreaming first. He ceased to shudder and his breath grew faint. He spoke, but his words made no sense. Hult reached gently into his consciousness and found all confused within. He touched the tenuous filaments of a mood and traced his way deeper into Sholot's mind, instilling wordless peace and calm as life faded around him. When the final silence came, he withdrew and turned to Beleg. She was stronger, and when their minds met he sensed such determination that he was certain she would overcome. But all at once, she broke; the strength within her dissipated like cloudrack and the silence closed on Hult's solitude. He left her mind and sat by their bodies for a time. He felt compassion, which was new to him.

He dutifully arranged their limbs in a sitting posture and faced them to Starside. He drew a fireblock from his robes, ignited it with a twist of his huge fingers, and set the dreamfire equidistant between them, the third point of a triangle that made an arrowhead into the deeper darkness.

For a time he sat by them, his mind opened fully to theirs; but they were still. They had gone too soon to leave anything behind. He thought of the tribe, slaughtered; the young, diminished by mischance and now by the shaking sickness; himself, in nithbrog and unable to bring new life to the tribe, only to guide and protect those already living; and he felt a great emptiness.

Then, into his receptive mind, there came a cold presence. He drew it in, examined it, and remembered. This was the consciousness of the little band of humans who did not act like the others. They were the impenetrable ones. And they were near.

Even if he could not penetrate their minds, he could range them and follow their movements. He did so, and found that they were at the campsite from which all had fled. They were motionless, and none of the fearful ones were with them.

Hult had to know more. He had the young back, but humans were always a danger, and these were too near. They might even be in pursuit. He reached out, and subtle tendrils of psychic force touched those opaque and clouded minds and groped diligently for entry.

Some were sleeping, and only a few remained awake; Hult could determine that much. He moved in all their minds, seeking but not finding. And then, as if a key had suddenly turned in a stubborn lock, all lay open to him.

In these humans there was no fear and no desire. They were unaware of his presence. Hult sensed powerful loyalties; extreme destructive urges banked, now, like sleeping fires, but ready to blaze up into holocaust under stimulation; iron self-discipline and self-control, even to the point of death. They were human, and in them lay all the complexity of humanness, and yet somehow all was clear and simple in their consciousness.

Hult went deeper, and discovered that they had been made this way. Others had done this to them, and they had submitted willingly.

He withdrew from them, shaken at the new knowledge of humans. What they had done to his tribe was no worse than

the things they did, and allowed to be done, to themselves
and to one another. He felt a great pity for such creatures,
at once so strong and so weak, and with the pity was mingled deep dread for what these truncated minds might lead
them to do. They were capable of anything.

More sensations he had never known before . . . compassion, pity, loneliness, and now fear. The onset of nithbrog
and the burgeoning of new powers brought terrible pangs.
The price of inner wisdom was high.

Hult did not think long on his problems. He reached out
to the tribe, and all were well. Dengar led the way and
Narik guarded the rear. One by one he touched minds with
the others, and they were reassured.

All but Roilan, whose mind flickered for an instant, like
the skyblaze on the Brightside horizon. Hult held, without
communicating, but the flickering passed and there was only
the thought of food and rest close ahead and a dulled
awareness of the sledge straps taut against Roilan's shoulder, and Themle pulling at his side. All might be well.

He left them and turned again to the humans. Now he
knew the way into their consciousness, and knew that they
remained unaware of his visitation. He intruded cautiously,
penetrating layer after layer of barriers, seeking knowledge
of their mission.

Tassur had risen halfway through the last watch. He inspected the food packs stacked carefully on the sledge, and
was pleased. More here than he'd expected. The haxopods
were sleeping soundly, rolled into mounds of thick fur.
Their breathing was barely noticeable under the shaggy
coats. That's the sort of insulation it takes to live in Starside,
he reflected. They'll sleep in one place for a full watch, and
the ice won't be melted under them.

It will be good to have this mission behind me, he
thought. Third coldworld mission I've been on, and that's

enough for any man. I'm about due for a training stint on
Occuch, and maybe then they'll send me somewhere hot
and dry. Even Xhanchos would be welcome, after this place.
Hot. Hot and dry, Xhanchos is, and that blue city . . . and
the pyramids, one beyond the other. . . .

With a start, he clutched at his wandering thoughts. This
was intolerable, on a mission so grave, with full respon-
sibility on his shoulders. He had never been one for day-
dreaming, and now was a poor time to begin.

Still angry at himself, he passed by a shelter and heard
the rustle of movement and a low mumble. He peered inside, but all within were still. Dreaming, that was all.

But men on Nolo do not dream. Nor does a Sternverein
combat officer lose himself in reverie with a mission before
him. There was an alien force at work in his mind. Something was affecting them all; not with terror, like the others,
but with distraction. And in Starside, distraction was
deadly.

Tassur decided at once. There was no time to spare. They
had to track that Onhla monster down and kill it, kill them
all and their beasts with them, and take back those gorwol
pelts. He turned to the shelters. The troop must be roused at
once.

Hult knew now why they had come, and that he must
stop them. Their weapons were too powerful to resist by
force, but he had a weapon of his own. He drove into their
minds, reaching for the proper skein of will and memory,
frantic to complete his work before all awoke and the collective consciousness was stronger and more able to resist.

He succeeded.

At Tassur's shout, the troopers of the Sternverein tumbled
from their shelters, weapons at the ready, and moved
smoothly into formation. Tassur saw it all happening, but

for an instant, he did not understand. Then all was clear, and he felt the anger surge into his will and tighten his voice. The fools! Incompetent, blundering, lazy fools!

"We've been sleeping like babies for over nine chronometer hours while the rest of our party is waiting back in Starside for these supplies!" he roared. "Now, let's get moving, and let's move fast! I want hot rations prepared at once. Shelters down, beasts saddled, sledge loaded. We move out immediately after first-meal. Do you understand?"

"Yes, sir!" came from eleven throats.

As they set about their duties, Graff said bemusedly to Casserio, "I wonder what set him off."

"I can't figure it. Didn't he order a ten-hour camp?"

Graff frowned, thought about the question, and then shook his head. "I don't remember. Did he?"

"I think so. Maybe. . . ."

"Maybe we assumed it. Tassur doesn't like long camps. He likes to keep moving once he's on a mission."

Casserio nodded. "That's right. That's absolutely right. By the blazing rings, then, where did we get the idea of a long camp? The Primary will have our hides for this!"

"The cold is getting to us. Our brains are freezing."

Hult stayed within their minds, but kept his presence enshrouded. He was aware of every thought that passed, but he revealed no sign of himself and they suspected nothing. He held until they had gone far along the track on which they had come, then he withdrew. They would not follow now. In their minds he and his tribe no longer existed, never had existed. The young were safe now. The Onhla would live.

Hult was satisfied. He rose and turned toward the caves of his tribe.

Along the way he passed the seated form of Roilan, facing into deep Starside and the long dreaming. Further on, in the same posture, was Themle. But the rest lived, and awaited him at the cave.

Tassur's men were upon the rendezvous before they recognized it. They saw no light and no sign of life. The beasts were gone, and the supply sledge stood empty.

Tassur ordered the troopers into covering positions. With two others, he rode into the campsite, and there he found the body of the Mission Primary.

Clell Basedow lay rigid, frozen through, face down on the icy ground. They turned him over, as one would turn a fallen statue, and both Kekring and Graff let out a gasp at the sight of the fireblock's effects. The left side of Basedow's chest was burned through to the bone, and a charred left shoulder cracked away with the movement of the body.

"What happened, Over-lieutenant? Where are the others?" Kekring asked.

Tassur knelt and pointed at a bit of white projecting from Basedow's chest, just under the breastbone. It was untouched by the heat. He reached down to where the body had lain and pried up the hilt of a dagger, snapped off clean from its blade. The two parts fitted.

"They killed him and ran off with the supplies. Kekring, get the others. Graff, start looking for their tracks. I'll send men to help you," Tassur said, without rising or looking up.

As they hurried off, he stood. He felt a sensation close to relief. Things were clear now. He had a mission fit for a Sternverein trooper, and he would not fail. The vague confusion that surrounded this entire expedition vanished as if a cold wind had swept all before it, and a single imperative blazed like a beacon in his memory: Mission Primary has been murdered: track down the murderers and destroy them. The Sternverein recognized no other justice, and the troopers were the dispensers.

As the others gathered data, the mission became ever more simple and straightforward. The dagger was Orm's;

they had all seen it in his hand when he ate. The other two were with him, and thus shared his guilt. All would be punished. No one, not even a king, laid violent hands on a Sternverein representative and lived to boast of it.

They camped, and beasts and men fed and rested to restore their strength. After first-meal, Tassur personally inspected each man's gear, and each beast. When he was satisfied, he assembled the troopers around the fireblock and addressed them.

"We came to Hraggellon as security forces for a trading mission. Now Mission Primary has been murdered, and our duty is to find and punish those who did it. That's a job better suited to us than ferrying sledges of food across Starside," he said, looking from one man to another as he spoke.

They nodded and voiced agreement, and he went on. "Each man will carry his own supplies. We'll leave the sledge and take the sledge animals as spare mounts. The sledge is too hard to pull at this temperature. It only slows us. Orm and his guardsmen have a good start on us, but they're traveling without spare mounts. They've left a clear trail. We should catch up to them within twelve long marches. Question, Casserio?"

"Their trail leads into Starside, Over-lieutenant—could that be a trick? Nobody in his right mind goes deeper into Starside, not even a fugitive. I can't understand why they even went this far. Doesn't it seem strange?"

Tassur hesitated a moment. Something vague and tenuous lay across his mind, like cobwebs blocking full clarity and memory. There was a reason why the expedition had come so far into this place of darkness and murderous cold. He frowned with the effort to recall it and snatched at the first glimpse of an answer.

"There's a trail, Casserio. . . . Orm spoke of a safe trail down along the Great Rift. He probably thinks we won't follow him any further into Starside . . . and he'll be able to beat us back to Norion and . . . set up an ambush. That's why he's going the way he did," Tassur said, growing more confident as he spoke.

The others took in his words, and looked at one another in momentary confusion. Then all became clear, and they muttered at their own obtuseness. Of course—Orm had spoken of the trail down the Great Rift—something to do with avoiding some natural danger—crevasses, that was it. Well, Orm would find that there were greater dangers, and no one escaped them. The Sternverein avenged its own. There was no escaping that.

"Very well, then," Tassur resumed, and they fell to attentive silence. "We'll follow the trail at the best pace we can manage. Once we catch up to them, we'll have extra food and mounts, so the trip back to Norion will be easier. Now, strike this camp and load up. We leave at once."

Two full darks after the departure of the joint force, not one Sternverein participant had returned. Only known survivors were seven native Hraggellian guardsmen, three of whom died before reaching Norion. The others . . . gave a garbled account of . . . inexplicable paralyzing terror that overcame them suddenly and caused them to scatter in panic.

No information is available regarding the whereabouts, or continued survival, of Primary, security officer, or security troopers. A rescue expedition is . . . impossible to organize.

Kos Lalor, Tech One/Acting Primary

Fourteenth Hraggellian

XIII.

THE BEGINNING

Brinbel was the last of the cubs. Hult placed her beside the others, with her sightless eyes turned to Starside, and kindled the fireblock at her feet. He sat with her until the fireblock was cold ash.

It was long before he rose and turned his footsteps toward the cave. Narik and Dengar hung behind, following slowly in his track. Their spirits were low. They had felt the difference growing in their god-master as his kind dwindled, one by one, always from the same shivering, wasting blight that struck them down without warning, and they were troubled.

They did not fear death; the shaking sickness took none but Onhla. Nor did they ever fear that Hult might succumb; gods do not die. He would remain, guiding, infusing wisdom and courage, providing. But he had changed, and they were uneasy at what further change might bring. Hult was not present to them as he once had been. Even now, he no longer joined them on the hunt. They could still sense him moving in and out of their minds in quick flashes as they struck past the slashing horns of a tulk, or closed on one of the bloated sea creatures, cutting off its escape and trapping it on the ice for a quick and easy kill. But he was not physically by their sides, not before their eyes and present to their scenting.

And even as they thought this, Hult was with them, flowing like warmth through their veins, and they knew all would be well. There was new life in Dengar. The koomiok would live on, and the hunting would be ever better. Filled with vigor, the two beasts loped off smoothly to stalk a great prize for Hult.

Hult ranged them for a long distance. They were the last

living remnant of his tribe, and he was reluctant to be long without them.

Now, with the last cub in the long dreaming, Hult was alone as no other creature had ever been, for now there was no future. The Onhla were gone from Hraggellon forever. No other planet would ever re-engender them. He relived that time, so many darks ago, when he had thought himself alone; now it was irrevocably so; nothing could change it. No otherworlder's ship would take him to a place of legend. All was ended now.

What pained him was not loneliness. Those in nithbrog grew accustomed to life within a citadel of body that enclosed an ever-expanding universe of mind. Alone, he was not lonely; he could never be lonely again, for he had become a part of all around him and knew a oneness with his world that he had never imagined possible.

Through both his earlier life-phases, he had felt little beyond the necessity of the moment. As a cub, his life had been the hunt and the tormagon-bond. In haldrim, he had sought and found a partner, that they might create and nurture a new tribe to keep the Onhla ways alive; nothing else mattered then. But he had endured the final metamorphosis, and now all the knowledge of the planet lay open to him; the minds of the dreamers who had gone before surrounded him like a nourishing sea of wisdom, and he became one with them in a synthesis that unraveled the ancient lore of the Onhla, perceiving and comprehending what once had been unfathomable.

He knew now why his people distrusted words and spoke seldom to one another and barely at all to outsiders. In the full understanding of nithbrog, all other attempts at communication were revealed as primitive and inadequate gropings; the dim foreknowledge of this curbed the Onhla's tongues.

It was not alone with the dreaming elders that Hult enjoyed communion. He was a filament in the web of planetary life and thought and feeling, now and in the past and future, in forgotten times and in times not yet imagined. All was one with him, and he was in all, a part of all.

In him, mixed with the pulsing of his own body, beat the complex rhythms of Hraggellon, and of the living things around him and the stars overhead. On this world that knew no music, he quickened to an unending symphony in which he was at once audience, player, and instrument.

Hult rode the winds that swept the world: the harsh pundergorn, bringer of frost and darkness; the galendergorn, daughter of light and lifebringer to the dwellers within walls; the brutal chedgorn, uprooter and floodmaker; even the dreaded gornthagorn, the wind that roared from nowhere once in many lifetimes and leveled all before it. He was one with the nameless gentle breezes that brushed the grainfields at harvest; one with the eternal rivers of wind that circled Hraggellon high above, and with their counterparts below, the currents that scoured the sea bottoms and churned at the edges of the land, biting and disgorging, destroying and building and never resting. He shared the tranquility of the open seas and the slow shifting of the huge rock plates that drifted across Hraggellon's semimolten mantle to clash with ponderous majesty in encounters that made the planet groan.

He partook of the life all around him. Not merely his own koomiok, but all that lived was in his ken. He knew the darktime slumber of the sunseekers, their slow awakening to the faint gleam, and then the hungry time of craving, and the onset of satiety, and the growing lethargy as the sun dropped ever lower and the shadows lengthened. He felt the thin impersonality of the grainfield multitudes, the quiet strength of the firebloom, the straining hunger of the heatthief. He knew the brute anger of the tulk, the fear of the gorwol, the exhilaration of the ice-skimmer; all living things bared their inmost life at his touch. Even the unseen, immeasurable giants that lived and moved in the crushing darkness at the bottom of the seas, oblivious to the land and all upon it, became a part of him.

He experienced sensations no human mind had ever conceived of, feelings for which no words existed in his language or any other; those without such feelings would have found words meaningless, and those who felt had no need of words. Hult felt all, and knew, and with his knowledge came sadness.

It was a dead knowledge; an end; it would go no further. He had achieved nithbrog, and now there was no need for him. He had no tribe.

The ancients had always been difficult to understand, and now he knew the reason. Their minds could not accommodate themselves to the meager universe of nine senses and a slumbering mind, a life swept helplessly from past to future with all slipping by untasted, unlearned, unknown. Those in nithbrog tried to reach out, but even in total contact, they could not give what was beyond another's capacity to receive. And so the elders wove the knots of wisdom, and the others groped for their meaning, hoping for the day when they, in nithbrog, might read with knowing fingers; and those few who came to nithbrog found that the knots were no longer needed. They knew, and the knots they had tied before seemed childish scribblings.

Something—perversity, perhaps; or fear, or hope, or the ineluctable weight of ageless tradition—nevertheless induced each elder to add to the knotted annals. It might even be that this was their purpose, for Hult, alone, with none to receive his words, none to read the knots he handed on, still wove the intricate patterns in strips of hide.

It was hope that drew him on. And hope, for him, now, was an act of madness. Yet he did not cease to hope.

For two full darks he remained in the caves, rarely venturing forth. He ate little now; his source of nourishment was elsewhere. His journeying was not of the body; he moved into his own deepening powers, into a past that was no longer unattainable, a future that opened with crystalline clarity, a penetration of all life and being. Time fell away. Hope remained. The strip of knots grew ever longer.

When Dengar gave birth, Hult emerged from himself and was one with the koomiok, deep within their minds, strengthening and comforting, easing the pains of the dam, the sudden terror that filled the nascent cubs, the confusion of Narik at the transforming of his mate. The beasts and the Onhla were one for a time, as before, and Narik and Dengar and their fat furry cubs enjoyed the glory of Hult's closeness with a joy beyond expression. Then Hult retreated to his inner life.

At the end of the second dark he felt the convergence of events that marked a turning point. Drawing all his powers to himself, he rose.

Shaelecc's band numbered ninety-six. They had lost many along the weary way, and now only the strongest and the most valuable were left.

Syger had died during the first Starside encampment, and many had died with him, some from the cold, some from starvation. The survivors had learned much from that time of suffering, and they entered the second long encampment with trebled supplies. Even so, a fifth of their number died. For all they knew, these ninety-six were the only Remembrancers alive on Hraggellon.

Starside had taken a heavy toll, and might yet claim more. But they could not turn back; what lay behind them was worse. Their enemy was a fierce and brutal race. Reduced in number as they were, the Remembrancers could not hope to resist by force, even if they were skilled in battle. Beyond Starside might be a haven. They could hope for no other, and so they persevered.

The way was uncertain, and they were often lost. All sledges had been abandoned. With their beasts reduced to fewer than a score, and these needed to carry Shaelecc and the sick and their supplies, and to provide mounts for the scouts, progress was slow in the brief times of travel. Every step seemed to drain the strength of a long march. Only the hope of sanctuary drew them on. After the hardship would come a place where they could settle, and remain, and not fear an enemy that might descend from nowhere and slaughter them for an unknown reason.

But when they came upon the frozen men, their spirits were shattered. They were plunged into confusion and despair.

They had at last reached the Great Rift, and were making their way to its head, deep in Starside. Tolomors, one of the evodes, had recited memories of a legend which told of a river that led from the head of the Rift, through Starside, into an enormous sea that never froze. The tale was ancient, predating even the Forgotten Darks. All agreed that it must be an allegory; but it was possible that the allegory had some foundation in fact, and so they sought the river.

The way along the Rift was terraced by ice ledges that rose in strata about twice the height of a man. The Remembrancers traveled on the second level, below the blasts from the windy surface. Three more levels dropped like steps between them and the Rift, but they thought this level to be the most prudent. The Rift was deep, and the ledges were treacherous. The second level was sufficiently sheltered, yet safe.

Abruptly, Ronlef and Tenik, the advance scouts, returned along the narrow pathway in great haste, heedless of danger. Ronlef rode directly to Shaelecc's side and sprang from his mount to speak; Tenik had halted ahead to bar the way. Ronlef reported their find to the leader. Upon hearing it, Shaelecc ordered the caravan to turn back to a suitable campsite at once. She sent two hunters ahead to relieve Tenik and ordered the rest of the able-bodied to pitch camp as soon as possible. This was a matter to be decided in council.

A few old familiars still sat in council, but now there were many young among them. This journey had been hard on the old. Shaelecc, propped up and sunk deep into her heavy furs, bid the scouts speak, and Ronlef stepped forth to speak for both.

"At a wide spot on the ledge, we found frozen bodies of three otherworlders. One of them held in his hand this small speaking machine. In Norion they call it a 'soundscriber.' All were armed," Ronlef said, displaying the instrument and pausing for questions.

"Were they in ambush?" Shaelecc asked.

"I think not. We saw no food, and the three were in a single shelter, in closed sleeping gear. Their bodies were much wasted. We believe they became lost, ran out of food, and died."

"When?" an evode asked.

"We cannot say."

"You call them otherworlders. Explain," Shaelecc said.

"Their bodies are human, but they differ slightly from ours. They carry weapons unlike any on Hraggellon, and are dressed in black, like the otherworlders who rode with Orm. The soundscriber is an artifact from off Hraggellon, and the clothing they wear is different from ours. It is not fur, but a soft metal, flexible as skin. It was not made on Hraggellon," Ronlef explained. "And their speech is not of this planet. Hear it."

He dropped to one knee, balanced the little soundscriber on his level thigh, and depressed a plate with strange markings. A voice came forth, weak but clear, and they listened in reverent and uncomprehending silence to the dead man's message:

"Over-lieutenant Tassur, Security Officer, Fourteenth Hraggellian . . . final report.

"Orm is dead, executed for the murder of Mission Primary Basedow. The justice of the Sternverein stands unblemished. . . .

"Casserio, Graff, and I have chosen this place to die. Too weak to go on. Behind us lie nine men of the Sternverein, buried according to their customs and our strength. Know that we did our duty, and die without regret. . . ."

The soundscriber clicked off of its own accord. For some time, no one spoke. At last Shaelecc said, "Their speech is unknown to us, but we heard the name of Orm. I suggest that it is reasonable to hold that these are some of the other-worlders who rode with Orm's guardsmen to attack our brothers."

"Then Orm is ahead of us!" an evode cried.

"We believe these three were lost," Ronlef said.

"Do lost men wander ahead of their companions? No, Orm awaits ahead—we must turn back!" the old man said.

"But Orm and his men may be behind us," said another.

"Perhaps Orm and his men are dead, too, and these were the last survivors," a woman suggested.

"Perhaps. How can we know?"

In the silence that followed, Shaelecc said, "We cannot know. We must decide, and take the risk."

The council continued. Discussion became heated, and then grew acrimonious. Anger had never before been the way of Remembrancers, but their ways had changed. Fear and despair assailed them as never before. Even the wisest elders could not contain their bitterness at this final blow to their hopes. Orm's guardsmen and their otherworld helpers meant death. Were they behind them, closing in even now? Or were they camped ahead, in ambush, waiting to fall upon the hapless caravan at some bend in the trail? They might be closing in from both directions. And even without Orm's brutality, the cold of Starside was killing them slowly; given time, it would claim them all.

Orm would follow forever. The cold would never end. There was no escape, no refuge. Voices rose, and some cried, "Turn back! Orm waits ahead, we must turn back!" Others shouted, "We must go on! Orm is drawing closer!"

Some were silent, numb with despair, crushed by the futility
of a choice between the certain deaths that waited on all
sides. One varasdode said, "Better to plunge into the Rift
now, and have done with our suffering," and some stood to
second his words.

Shaelecc listened and watched, and bowed her head in silence. She had brought them far. Now, it seemed, they
could move no farther. This was the breaking point. She had
never lost faith in the stories of a land beyond the darkness,
but she knew that once divided, the Remembrancers would
never reach it. To have come so far, and then to destroy
themselves from fear . . . she could not permit that.

"We must go on! We will go on!" she cried, her thin voice
cutting through the babel.

A varasdode turned to confront her. "No, we will not. We
need a new leader—one who can lead us to safety, not destruction."

"A new leader!" The cry went up from several throats,
and at once brought forth a countercry of loyalty to Shaelecc. Ronlef, Tenik, and three young hunters stepped to her
side, their weapons drawn, and formed a defensive ring
around her. Elsewhere in the tent, other weapons were
drawn. All were silent. The two armed groups tensed and
slowly shifted into position, each awaiting the other's move.
The elders shrank back against the wall of the tent and held
their tongues. They saw that their authority was gone,
passed to the wielders of weapons.

It seemed to Shaelecc that the end had come. There had
been signs and warnings, but she had not heeded, giving
herself instead to a foolish hope. Now in one frozen moment
of time it was all obvious. The slow decay had begun with
the turn to Starside, and only now could the results be seen.
The Remembrancers had become like those who pursued
them; they were their own enemy.

Memories were crumbling; evodes were dying, or growing ill and feeble, before they could pass on their full store

to a disciple. The young, for their part, were losing interest in the past and turning to a life of action and immediacy. They wished to learn only what would make them better hunters. The ancient game of dur-ron-ag had been abandoned. Some were concerned, but many were openly glad, for they had come to consider the game a waste of time and strength. Men were made to hunt and provide, these said, and a life spent seated among silent gamesters ruminating on the mental manipulations of other gamesters long dead was foolish and wasteful.

The decay accelerated. The evode Jara died suddenly, and with him vanished the legends of the earliest dwellers in shadowlands. A sledge broke through the fragile covering of a crevasse, taking two paturdodes and two mendodes in its wake; the law and healing knowledge of nine tribes was lost with them.

And now Shaelecc saw Remembrancers prepared to shed one another's blood. It had come to this, and none seemed able to stop the headlong rush to savagery. She cried out with all her waning strength, but a mocking gust of wind drummed across the tent top, drowning her appeal, and no one heard.

Over her, and over all within the tent and all who waited disconsolately outside, despair fell like a pall. They felt a darkness of the spirit deeper than the darkness that lay over the heart of Starside.

And then, like the coming of firstlight to their old homes, a peace came over them and they knew that all was well. Their enemies were dead, and the dead were enemies no longer. They were secure from Orm and all who would pursue them. A new home lay ahead, and they would be brought to it safely, in honor.

The rebellious varasdode dropped his weapon and bowed low before Shaelecc's beaming face. "Shaelecc is our leader, and she will decide for us," he said humbly.

His supporters followed his lead. The little group of

guards laid their weapons aside and stepped forward to raise the others and embrace them in peace. In the tent, under the blows of a rising wind, a flood of peace and certainty and unity suffused all present. It spread beyond, an invisible, irresistible tide, and the huddled fugitives rose and looked at one another in joyous wonder.

"Shaelecc is our leader. Be it thus remembered," said the oldest of the evodes.

Shaelecc's voice arose, weary but filled with content. "My leadership is nearly ended. A new leader comes, to take us to our goal."

Hult strode forward over the frozen ground, toward the Great Rift, and the royal beasts of his tribe slipped like shimmering shadows encircling him. He had learned much from the dreamers, and now all his wisdom had a purpose.

Onhla identity was deeper than mortal flesh and blood and bones. Bodies died, but the Onhla might live on; and now, with all bodies dead but one, they would live where sickness and hatred could not assail them. The Onhla lived in their lore and legendry, the memories, the deeds, the wishes of accumulated generations; in the tales of Blademaker and the First Walkers, the marvels of Lathpen the Blind, and the long acclamations of the Maker of Weathers; in the rituals of Great Gathering, and the training of the hunting packs, and the knotting of the past. Let a new tribe embrace all these, and the new tribe, whatever their past, whatever their colors, would be Onhla.

Hult drew to himself the minds of the dreaming generations, and cast that mighty consciousness far ahead in greeting. From the Remembrancers he gleaned an outpouring of glad anticipation.

In his solitude, Hult had learned that it was possible to touch human minds in many ways, on many levels. In the minds of these humans, he had found fear, but also courage and a will to survive, and a love of all things past. And no

H 42

hatred. Most important of all, he had felt need, and it was a need that matched his own.

The ones who had killed were dead and silent. He ranged their frozen presence, and there was nothing in them. Those few who had survived from the band of marauders had returned from the cold places gibbering of horrors. They would never return to Starside. His new people were safe from them, and once he had led them across the frozen sea to the home of the gorwol, they would be safe forever.

They would live; the Onhla would live. The knots of wisdom would be tied by different hands, but the last knot lay far in the future.

EPILOGUE

Final Entry
Pending an official investigation into the fate of the Fourteenth Mission, all contact with the world named Hraggellon is to cease.

Effective this date, Hraggellon is a quarantined world to all driveships of the Sternverein.

Star charts are to be marked in accordance with this directive.

Norin Holoman-Leddendorf

Supreme Commander, Sternverein Fleet